Will Allen conquered his fears and has become a Monster Detective!

But in his very first case, will he be skilled enough to save himself and his friends from a Monster more terrifying than his most dreadful imaginings?

…Suddenly, spears of fire began to strike the ground all around us.

"Run!" Timmy cried as he stumbled back. "Head for the fort!"

"No!" I shouted, grabbing him by the shirt and pulling him back. "You have to stand up to it…"

At just that moment, I screamed as a burst of flame shot through the air and scorched my shoulder, burning a huge, searing hole in my jacket. I looked down at my smoldering coat, and then up at Timmy, who was still tangled in my grasp. We stared blankly at each other for a second.

"Um, new plan," I muttered as more jets of fire shot out at us. *"Run for your life!!!"*

ISBN 10 : 0-9789512-2-0
ISBN 13 : 978-0-9789512-2-1

Library of Congress Catalog # 2008927392

Illustrations copyright © 2009 by Jeffrey Friedman
Text copyright © 2009 by Jeffrey Friedman

All rights reserved. Published by Rogue Bear Press.

First Printing - Halloween 2009

Printed in the U.S.A.by BookMasters, Inc.
30 Amberwood Parkway, Ashland, OH 44805
Date of printing 9/09
Job number M6416
Tracking Information Code : 951221 – 1a
CPSC Product Tracking Information available at
http://roguebearpress.com/custom4.html

This book is rated **level II** in the **Rogue Bear Press** *AcceleReader* Program. It is designed for children 7-14 years of age.

Learn more about our *AcceleReader* Program at our website, **RogueBearPress.com.**

Teachers and Librarians take note :

Special sales discounts are offered to schools and libraries. Discounts are available for purchases of as little as 5 copies.

Check our website for details about our discount program.

Will Allen
and the
Ring of Terror

JASON   EDWARDS

Rogue Bear Press
New York

Books by JASON EDWARDS:

The Chronicles of the Monster Detective Agency:

Will Allen and the Great Monster Detective

Will Allen and the Ring of Terror

Will Allen and the Hideous Shroud

Will Allen and the Terrible Truth

Will Allen and the Unconquerable Beast

Will Allen and the Dubious Shrine

Will Allen and the Lair of the Phantoms

Will Allen and the Greatest Mystery of All

Because *Jenna* and *Jessica*
provided the inspiration;

Because my *Wife* and my *Father*
have made everything possible;

and because **you**, the readers,
give me a reason to keep at it.

The story goes on...

Contents

Monster Detective Agency
Will Allen
Detective Third Class
Jeannine Fitsimmons
Chief Executive
Specializing in identification and eradication
of all types of ghouls and beasties
Fee Negotiable

Chapter One – Introductions

You know, when you're being hung upside down from your ankle by a gruesome tentacle while slobbering fangs are shooting out at you from every direction, there really is room for only one thought in your panic-stricken brain.

"How do I get myself into these things?" I grumbled as a pair of vicious, fanged jaws came flying right at my face.

Now I know that may seem like a bit of an unusual situation to find yourself in, but you see, my name is Will Allen, and I'm a monster detective.

Yes, you read that right: I'm a *monster detective*. And no, I'm not pulling your leg, or talking about some fantasy role-playing game. I fight monsters. The big, slobbery, use your head as a chew toy kind. Now, I know 5th graders like me aren't supposed to believe in stuff like that anymore, but I can tell you for sure that there definitely are monsters out there. I should know. Not long ago, I myself had some monsters under my bed.

Yes, I mean *real* monsters, and no, I wasn't just imagining things.

Now I happen to be one of the smartest kids in my school, but I was having trouble figuring out what to do about the monsters until a strange business card appeared in my book bag. The card belonged to Bigelow Hawkins, the Great Monster Detective, and he gave me a special spyglass and flashlight and taught me how to use them to defeat the monsters. Well, I don't mean to brag, but I was so good at fighting monsters that Bigelow suggested that I should become a monster detective myself. So then the next thing you know, there I was, about to be eaten alive.

Wait, I'm kind of jumping ahead a bit, aren't I? Sorry. If you really want to know how I ended up like that, let's go back just a little, O.K.?

First of all, let me tell you that starting your own business is not easy. It's a lot of work, not the least of which is trying to convince your parents that you have to be allowed to stay out past your bedtime to do your job. It's one of the many complications you face when you're starting up a monster detective agency.

"Don't miss your curfew tonight," my mother warned in her *or you'll be in big trouble* tone of voice as I tip-toed across the hallway to our front door. I froze in my tracks, and looked back toward the kitchen to find her staring down at me.

"How did you…" I began, but my mom cut me off.

"And what in the world are you doing in those ratty old clothes?" she asked, eyeing the trench coat and bowler hat that I'd stolen out of the attic with a look of disgust on her face.

"It's my uniform," I replied, pointing at the silver medallion pinned on the top left side of my coat. "Can't you read my badge? It says: Monster Detective Agency, Detective Third Class! I'm on my way to Timmy Newsome's house to solve my very first…"

"Never mind!" my mother interrupted curtly. "Just be home by eight o'clock, or you'll be grounded for a week."

I frowned. You see, the problem with that is monsters don't come out during the daytime, which means I had to wait until dark to get started, so it was already late.

"But mom," I protested. "I might not be finished doing my...you know, my *job* by then."

That put her in a bit of a snit.

"Your silly charade will be over when I say so," she answered.

Mothers just don't understand free enterprise.

"That's not fair!" I complained. "You don't punish dad when *he* has to work late."

For some reason, she grinned slyly at that.

"Oh, you think so?" she said.

Now as any kid knows, arguing with a mom is totally useless. Especially when she's dead wrong about something. Of course, that never stopped me before, but I had a job to get to, and time was wasting, so I gave in.

I really hate doing that.

"Okay," I grumbled through gritted teeth. "Eight o'clock then."

My mother smiled smugly, which just made it worse. I took out my flashlight, the special one called the *RevealeR* that had been given to me by Bigelow Hawkins, and pointed it at my mother, but when I flicked the switch, it had no effect.

"Well, this really stinks!" I grumbled to myself. "What good is a monster-fighting flashlight that won't work on *moms*?"

"What was that?" my mom asked.

"Ah, nothing," I said, thinking as I did that the next time I had a job, I'd tell my mom I was going for a sleepover.

It was already dusk when I left the house. The little color that was left on the autumn leaves still clinging to their branches had faded into a strange, murky mist that drifted menacingly through the trees. Bits of the eerie fog reached out in all directions like fingers looking for something to strangle.

You know, spooky stuff like that used to make my hair stand on end like a cat that just had its tail stepped on, but now that I know that there really are monsters out there, it doesn't bother me at all.

Hey, don't ask me to explain it: I'm a detective, not a psychiatrist.

"Silly charade!" I growled into the syrupy air as I walked to Timmy Newsome's house. "She called it a silly charade! I'd like to see *her* face a monster or two! Then let's see what she called it!"

Of course, I knew that was impossible. Bigelow taught me that monsters are fears that have come to life, and that adults can't really understand kids' fears, so they don't even *see* our monsters. Personally, I think that if monsters personify our fears, my mother couldn't see one unless it looked like a dent in the fender of her car, or a big stain in the middle of her Persian Rug.

That dark, swirling mist seemed to follow me every step of the way to Timmy's house. It swallowed the stars, the moon, and the light from the streetlamps as it crept across the sky, and spat out a shadowy haze all around me.

"13...15...17..." I counted as I passed each mailbox. "Ah, here we are! 23 Secor Lane."

I looked up from the mailbox to see Timmy's house, which was glowing darkly in the light of the hazy cloud. It was bigger than my house, with a huge terrace hanging out over the driveway of the two-car garage, and was surrounded by large, untrimmed hedges. The outer walls were covered in climbing vines, and the grounds were bordered by a white picket fence with faded, peeling paint. The gloomy cloud overhead fell across the cracked stone path leading to the front door and perched itself along the crown of the house as I approached. It would be hard to explain how, but I could just *feel* that there was something evil lurking in that house. I took a deep breath and boldly stepped through the gate, which creaked loudly as it opened, but I was still shooting an occasional glance upward when I rang the bell. A woman with an upturned nose and hair pasted with enough gel to hold back a rhino answered the door. Her frozen scowl and perfectly manicured claw-like nails reminded me a little bit of my great aunt Martha, and a little bit of a pterodactyl.

"Yes?" she said, eyeing me like I was a load of toxic waste dumped on her doorstep.

"I'm Will Allen," I answered in my most professional tone of voice. "I'm here to help Timmy with his..."

"...My math homework!" Timmy shouted as he dashed down the stairs in our direction. He stopped at the door and bent over, panting. His long red hair spilled over his big, round glasses, making him look a lot like Poindexter from the *Rocky and Bullwinkle Show*.

No, I'm not making that up. If you've never heard of him, you obviously haven't been watching the Classic Cartoon Channel.

"Will's a whiz at math, mom," he said breathlessly.

I just fixed him with one of my patented '*say what?*' looks. I mean, I *am* a whiz at math, but I don't think that's likely to be very helpful when dealing with some giant, slobbering squid, saber-toothed purple gorilla, or whatever it was that might be lurking in Timmy's room.

"Oh! Well, do come in," his mother said in a suddenly gracious tone. Her scowl eased, but the lines from it remained etched in her face. Timmy ushered me quickly through the foyer and up the stairs to his room.

"We'll be working in my room, mom," he called out as he shoved me through the door. "Tell dad that's where I'll be."

"Timmy," his mother called back in a strangely exasperated voice, "You know your father..."

But Timmy slammed the door before she could finish. He looked up at me nervously as I scanned all around his room. There was nothing clearly monstrous about it, unless you count the fact that it was unnaturally clean and tidy, but it was definitely not a normal-looking kid's room either. The furniture and decorations were all old, antique stuff, like they came from a museum or something. As I scanned the walls, I noticed that they were lined with lot of fancy, framed pictures, but none of them were of Timmy. Along the far side wall there was a roll-top desk with lots of drawers labeled with strange words on them, and a matching end table with a phone on top was sitting in the corner near the closet door. Sticking out into the middle of the room from the wall opposite the closet was a big four post bed with a canopy on top. To look at this room, you'd think that it was the guest room at a fancy inn, not the home of an eleven year old boy.

"So," Timmy said, "Do you really think you can help me?"

"If you can handle your monster as rough as you did me," I answered tartly, "you won't *need* any help."

Now you have to understand, I get a little upset about being shoved around, seeing as how I'm one of the shortest and scrawniest kids in my grade. I always have been, owing to my being at least a year younger than almost everyone else.

Timmy, who stood nearly a head taller than me, bit his lip.

"Look, I'm sorry about that, okay?" he said.

"I just don't want my mom to know what's going on."

"Why not?"

"Because…" he sputtered, "because she thinks it's all a dream or something. She took away all my comic books, because she said they must be causing me nightmares. Then she sent me to a shrink!"

"A what?"

"A psychiatrist! She doesn't understand. My monster is *real*. Who knows what she'll do if she finds out what you're *really* here for?"

"So you told your parents that I'm a...a math tutor?"

"Yes!" he said, grabbing my shirt urgently. "So, can you help me or not?"

I pulled myself out of his grip.

"Relax," I told him. "If I couldn't help, my card wouldn't have appeared in your book bag."

"That reminds me," he said, scratching his head just like Jeannine Fitsimmons, my best friend and partner, always does. "I was meaning to ask you: how did you do that? How did you put that card in my bag without me seeing you? And for that matter, how did you even know I have a monster?"

"I *didn't* know," I explained. "But the *card* did."

Timmy gave me a squinty kind of look. He reached into his pocket and pulled out a small rectangle of paper that I instantly recognized was my

magic business card. He looked at it up and down
with the same squinty look.

"I don't get it," he finally said.

"Actually, neither do I," I answered. "Come
on, let's get to work."

Chapter Two – Echoes

The clock ticked loudly as we both just stood there silently in the middle of Timmy's room. The sound of it rebounded throughout the room, and seemed to get louder with each bounce.

"Well?" Timmy finally blurted.

I squirmed a little. Now that the time had come to begin my very first investigation, I felt a bit nervous. Fortunately, one thing I know for sure is that the secret to being a professional is to always *act* like you know what you're doing. I learned that from all the times I've seen my dad nod his head stupidly while his auto mechanic blabs a lot of gibberish at him.

"O.K.," I squeaked. I coughed, and then started again in a deliberately deep voice.

"O.K., the…um…the first thing we need to do is figure out what makes the monster appear." I said.

"Great," Timmy replied. "How do we do that?"

Um, I'm not really sure, I thought. But I wasn't going to tell Timmy that, so I bit my lip instead.

You see, I had never actually detected a monster by myself before. I'd only uncovered my own monster with Bigelow's help, so I fidgeted a bit, until finally an idea came to me.

Just do all the same things Bigelow did, I reasoned. *After all, they worked pretty well on **my** monsters.*

So I tried to do exactly what Bigelow had done when he first appeared. First, I pulled out my flashlight and magnifying glass, the special ones that Bigelow had given me, then I went to the light switch and turned it off. The room went dark, but some hazy moonlight filtered in through the mist surrounding the windows and gave everything around us an eerie blue glow.

"What did you do that for?" Timmy cried, his voice suddenly tense.

"We need for it to be dark," I explained. "That's the only way to lure out your monster."

"Then what's the flashlight for?" he asked.

"This flashlight is special," I said, holding it up for him to see. It was about six inches long with a dark red casing and tiny marks etched along the shaft. "It's called a **RevealeR**. It can shrink your monster until it's too small to scare you anymore."

Now I expected to hear a *WOW* or *Really? That's amazing!*

"Oh," was all he said. I looked at him, waiting for anything else to come out of his mouth, but he just shifted his gaze nervously around the room.

"So, where does the monster come at you from?" I finally asked.

"Over there," he answered, pointing to the corner of his room. There stood the closet door, and beside it the small end table with the telephone sitting on top. "They come out of the closet over there."

"I'll go check it out," I said boldly.

I walked on over, my magnifying glass pressed to my face, searching for signs of monsters. Inch by inch I crept, flashlight at the ready, to the closet door. There was no sign of anything strange in the sight of the glass, but the air became stale with the odor of rotting fish, growing more and more foul with every step I took. That made me edgy.

"I...I'm going in," I announced, and gently prodded the door.

Before I could even gasp, it flew open with a loud, creaking howl, and something dark and slimy fell upon me.

"YYYYYAAAAAAHH!" I screeched.

"YYYYEEEEAAAAAHH!" Timmy echoed

"OH MY GOD!" I shouted. "IT...IT'S SO HORRIBLE!"

"What is it?" Timmy cried. "What do you see?"

"What a *mess*!" I exclaimed, holding my nose as I gingerly lifted something that looked like a bunch of rotting banana peels off my coat. "And what a stink! Have you been using your closet as a trash bin?"

"It's the monster, you jerk!" Timmy bellowed.

"I don't think so," I shot back, examining the slimy mess carefully. "This is disgusting, but it's no monster. In fact, I don't see any monsters in here at all. No monster tracks, either."

"How can you see that?" Timmy asked.

"This isn't some plain old magnifying glass," I explained as I dropped the putrid scraps back into Timmy's closet, "It's a MonsterScope. It can...well, it helps me see stuff you can't see with just your eyes. *Monster* stuff, you know? But there's nothing in there. So, what's the deal?"

"Huh?" Timmy sputtered. "What do you mean?"

"I mean why am I looking at a closet full of rotting food that has no monster in it?"

"There *is* a monster," Timmy insisted. "There is!"

"I know that," I told him. "If there wasn't, you wouldn't have gotten my card. But what's all this mess about? *Really*?!"

I held my MonsterScope up and looked at him through it. Timmy suddenly cowered shyly, as though he thought that my glass could tell whether he was lying or not.

It can't, but of course Timmy didn't know that.

"All right, all right! That stuff is food I threw

in there to feed the monster, so it wouldn't eat me," Timmy confessed.

I looked back at the closet.

"It doesn't look like it likes your menu," I commented. "I guess your monster is a fussy eater."

Timmy threw his hands up in the air.

"Well then, what does it want?" he whined.

I thought a moment.

"I don't know," I answered. "That's what we need to find out."

I put away my flashlight and began scanning around the room with my MonsterScope, making a big, sweeping circle that started from the closet door and went all around the room.

Nothing.

"It might help me know what to look for," I suggested, "if you tell me more about the monster itself."

"Like what?" Timmy asked.

I tried to remember the questions Bigelow had asked me when he was searching for *my* monster.

I began by asking, "What do you see?" but Timmy just said, "*Nothing*, really. Just things moving around in the shadows sometimes. Mostly, I *hear* it."

"You hear it? Does it *say* anything?"

Now that might seem like a pretty simple question to you, but Timmy acted like I'd just asked if he still wore plastic undershorts.

"No!" Timmy yelled, suddenly enraged. "No it doesn't say anything! Just stop it! You're not helping!"

He looked so angry that I thought he might explode, but just then the phone on the end table rang, and he froze like a stone.

"Aren't you going to get that?" I asked.

Timmy didn't answer. He just stood there as the phone kept ringing. And ringing.

And ringing some more. I don't know how many rings it took before it occurred to me that there was something suspicious about it, but I decided to check it out. I walked back over to the end table and bent down to look at the phone more closely. To the naked eye, it appeared to be perfectly normal, but when I held my MonsterScope up and peered through the glistening glass, the receiver lit up with dozens of glowing spots.

"Yes! This is it!" I whispered excitedly. "Monster trails!"

"Timmy, I've found something!" I yelled. "I've found traces of the monster!"

"No! No you haven't!" he cried. "Just stop it! Get my dad! He's the only one who can help me!"

"But I..." I stammered.

"Get out!" Timmy screamed. "Just leave me alone and get out!"

At this point, I was feeling a bit unappreciated. But I am a monster detective, and a monster detective doesn't give up, even when his client is even weirder than any monster. I was determined to do my job, so I pulled my special flashlight back out and pointed it at the phone.

"Um, we should really see where these trails lead…" I insisted.

But when I flicked the switch on the RevealeR, nothing happened.

"Uh oh. This is bad..." I mumbled, smacking the casing with my hand.

"You see!" Timmy shouted. "You're useless! Now just go!"

"But the ringing…"

"Never you mind about the ring! It's none of your business!"

This whole thing was getting a little freaky, even by monster detective standards.

"I didn't say *ring*. I said *ringing*," I bellowed.

"Aren't we going to do something about…"

But then I stopped speaking, because there, next to the phone, I suddenly spotted a golden ring.

"Wha…?" I mumbled to myself. "But…but that wasn't there a second ago."

Now, you don't have to be a genius or a monster detective to know that there's something strange about things that just appear from out of nowhere. So, naturally, I moved in close and held my MonsterScope up to check it out.

Through the glass, the ring lit up brightly with a kaleidoscope of colors and images. A sparkling steam arose from the entire golden band, which seemed to throb with hidden power.

"This…" I realized, "This is it! *This* is the monster!"

I smiled broadly, beaming with pride.

I've done it! I thought joyfully. *All on my own, I've detected a monster!*

But as I stared at the glowing band, my smile faded. I was actually kind of disappointed.

You see, after facing creatures like a giant flying shark, a humongous monster tree, and a ten-foot-tall man-eating toilet, this tiny little thing was something of a letdown.

What am I going to do? I thought morosely as I picked up the ring and looked it over. *There's not much point in trying to shrink this thing.*

Just then, the phone rang again. Except it wasn't the *phone* at all. With the ring held tight in my fingers, I could feel the band vibrate and shake as the sound emerged. The ringing sound was coming from *it*, not the phone.

"Well, *this* is annoying," I grumbled. I turned

back to Timmy, who recoiled like he had seen a...

...Well, something a lot scarier than a tiny little ring.

"This is it?" I asked, holding up the ring to Timmy's face. "This is your terrifying monster?"

Timmy stumbled back like I was trying to feed him Castor Oil.

"Shut up!" he shrieked. "Shut up and go away!"

"But I..."

"I mean it!" Timmy insisted. "Get out and leave me alone!"

For some reason, it seemed like a bad time to point out that I hadn't been paid yet. With my flashlight dead, and faced with a tiny little monster that did nothing but sit around making an annoying ringing sound, it didn't seem like there was much I could do anyway. I put the ring back down on the table and headed for the door, thinking as I did that at least I would be home in time for my curfew.

Chapter Three - Enlightenment

By the time I got back to my room I was feeling pretty irritated, especially since the first thing my dad said when I came in the door was, "So, how did it go tonight, detective boy?"

I don't know which was worse, my mother calling my profession a silly charade, or my dad trying to humor me. I grumbled something a little bit like, "detect *this*," as I stormed up the stairs. My dad called after me.

"I'm sorry," he bellowed, "but I couldn't quite make that out. Would it help if I got an English-Monster Language translator?"

Okay, I was wrong. I *do* know which was worse.

I slammed my door shut and plopped down in my chair. My foul mood grew as I took out my flashlight and looked it over. I flicked the switch, but nothing happened.

"Maybe the batteries are dead," I said to myself.

Hey, I'm not a detective for nothing. I opened the battery compartment, and my mouth dropped open.

There were no batteries at all.

"No wonder!" I sputtered. "Well, this should be easy to fix. I wonder if it takes AAs?"

"Not exactly," spoke a squeaky, yet gravelly voice.

I turned my head in the direction of the voice, which had come from an empty spot on my bed next to where my teddy bear sits.

Yes, I still have my Teddy Bear. No smart cracks about it, OK?"

As I watched, a bulge began to form under my blanket, which grew taller until it rose about three feet off my bed. From within, something tugged at the blanket, but since he had been standing on it, the blanket pulled his feet out from under him and the blanket-wrapped figure toppled over.

"Wooooff!" he coughed when he smacked into the floor with a thud. "Stupid blanket!"

I could see flailing and scratching going on underneath, so I yanked my blanket off the figure before it ended up torn to shreds. There, sprawled on the floor before me, was the Great Monster Detective, Bigelow Hawkins. He righted himself, ruffled his huge trench coat, and straightened his bowler hat.

"Hello, Will," He said cheerfully. "How's tricks?"

I was still in a bit of a mood.

"How's tricks?" I mimicked crossly. "Is that supposed to be funny?"

Bigelow backed away.

"Sorry," he said. "It's just a routine monster greeting."

"I…I'm sorry, Bigelow," I said. "It's just that I'm having a really rough night. I don't feel like a very good detective right now. Maybe I'm not cut out for this after all."

"Don't worry, Will. The first time is always the toughest. You'll get the hang of it."

"You really think so?"

"Of course! And I'm here to help," he announced eagerly. "So, what's the problem?"

"For starters, *this*," I said, shoving the flashlight at him. "This stupid flashlight!"

"You mean your *RevealeR*?" Bigelow corrected.

"Whatever!" I grumbled. "I don't know how to make it work!"

"Yes you do," Bigelow insisted. "It's just that it doesn't work simply because you *want* it to."

I rolled my eyes.

"Would you mind not speaking in riddles, please?" I asked.

"It's not a riddle," he maintained. "Can you tell me what the RevealeR does?"

"It…" I hesitated. "It shines light on monsters. It shrinks them until they can't hurt us anymore."

"Yes, of course," Bigelow agreed. "But as you already know, the monsters are simply fears that have come to life. How can a little light cause them to shrink?"

I thought back, remembering how my monsters had changed before my eyes when Bigelow shined the light on them.

"It reveals the truth about our fears," I whispered. "It shows them for what they really are, and makes them less scary."

"Very good, Will. Now, seeing the truth about monsters, or anything else for that matter, takes understanding. The light of understanding is one of the most powerful forces in the whole universe. But where do you suppose a light like that comes from?" Bigelow asked.

I thought for a moment, remembering the empty battery compartment. I looked down at my flashlight, which was warm and glowing in my hand.

"It...it comes from *me*," I said, looking back up at Bigelow. "That's it, isn't it? It comes from inside me."

"That's right," Bigelow encouraged. "Go on."

"So if I don't understand the monster," I reasoned, "then I have no light to shine on it?"

"Exactly," Bigelow explained. "So you see, the flashlight itself always works. But you need understanding..."

"...To make it light," I finished for him.

"You see?" he said with a smile. "You *are* a good detective."

But there was something else, something that had been nagging at me since Timmy brought it up back in his room.

"Bigelow, why did my business card show up in Timmy's book bag? How does it work?"

"You're a monster detective now," Bigelow reminded. "It works the same for you as it did for me."

"It just appears to those who need my help?" I asked.

"Of course," Bigelow confirmed. "The card knows when someone has a monster. *And* when they are ready for you to help them."

"But then why couldn't I help Timmy?"

"Don't worry," Bigelow smiled. "You will."

"How? Tell me what to do!" I pleaded.

Bigelow scratched his head, and I wondered to myself why, except for me, thinking makes everyone's head itch. Maybe it's because they're all allergic to it.

"There's only so much I can tell you," Bigelow explained. "And you already know most of it."

"Can't tell me more?" I complained. "Why? Are there monster lawyers out there checking up on you?"

"Oh, no," Bigelow mused. "No, we killed all

of those."

I'm *pretty* sure he was joking.

"No," he continued, "the reason I can't explain more is because there *is* no more to explain. You see, Will, every room, every monster, has its own set of rules, and it's up to you, the detective, to figure them out."

"So I have to figure out why a phone and a ring are Timmy's monsters," I reasoned. "Then I can use my flashlight to show the truth to Timmy, and make them less scary."

Bigelow just beamed.

"But what could be so terrifying about a tiny little ring?" I puzzled.

"That's what you have to figure out," Bigelow said. "When you do, your flashlight will be able to reveal the truth about Timmy's monster. The light of understanding will show you what it really is, and Timmy will be able to see it too. If he wants to."

"If he *wants* to?"

"Of course," Bigelow said. "You can't simply show Timmy the truth about the monster. It's not enough that he *can* see the truth. He has to *choose* to see it. And you must help him make that choice. Until Timmy chooses to face them, the monsters will just grow stronger."

"You mean…" I said hesitantly, "*I* can't fight them?"

"No, Will," Bigelow answered. "You're a detective, not a soldier. You can only act as a guide.

The only one who can defeat Timmy's monsters is Timmy himself."

"What if Timmy doesn't face them?" I asked nervously. "Could they grow big enough to...you know...devour us alive?"

"Monsters don't consume flesh," Bigelow explained, sounding a little annoyed. "They live by consuming something much more powerful than that. Something so strong that it can crush the will of the strongest men and paralyze entire armies in its devastating grip."

"Fear," I concluded. "They feed on our fears, don't they? That's why mine grew when I was afraid."

"Very good, Will," Bigelow said.

"But then wouldn't it be doubly frightening," I posed, "if a monster dispatched the fearless detective in some gruesome way right before Timmy's eyes?"

Bigelow seemed to be caught by surprise by that question.

"That can't happen," he said, but his squeaky voice sounded tense. "Don't worry, Will. If Timmy wasn't ready to face his monsters, the card wouldn't have appeared to him."

I wasn't convinced. But then Bigelow hadn't been in that room with Timmy, hadn't been ushered out of there like a skunk in a perfume factory.

"But Bigelow, Timmy kicked me out. He doesn't want my help anymore."

"He does," Bigelow insisted. "He is just very

afraid. Fear often makes us do foolish things. To defeat monsters, we must first master our fears."

"How do we do that?"

"Fear grips your body as well as your mind, Will. First take back control of your body, then you can free your mind," Bigelow instructed. "Begin by taking control of your breathing. Inhale deeply, and make your breaths slow and steady. Calm your breathing, and you will calm your mind. Then you can see past the fear and focus your thoughts on the task at hand."

I just stood there for a minute, thinking over all he had told me.

"Well, OK," I finally said, "I guess those are all the questions I have right now. Thanks for your help, Bigelow."

"No problem," he smiled in that toothy, monster way of his. "I'm always here if you need me. And just remember, Will: things are always less scary when you face them with a friend."

And with that, he pulled the blanket back over himself, climbed back onto the bed next to Teddy, and vanished.

Chapter Four – Sticky Subjects

If the night before had been a lousy one, the morning that followed quickly started to look even worse. For starters, my mom made breakfast. That may not sound so bad to *you*, but then you've never sampled my mother's cooking. Believe me; once you've tasted her notorious spinach and onion pancakes, you become a big fan of Tony the Tiger. After a short time spent stifling my gag reflex so that I could down a few bites, and a long time spent listening to my mom lecture me about the importance of a healthy diet, I dashed out the door late for my bus.

Again.

The last few kids were still stepping up the stairs of the bus as I sprinted to the bus stop. I ran up and jumped through the doors just as the driver began closing them, which caused me to land awkwardly on the second step and spill my books onto the floor. The bus driver scowled down at me as I knelt to pick them up.

"Thank you for joining us this morning," she

said sharply. "Now, find your seat! I've got a schedule to keep!"

I quickly stood myself back up, and when I finally raised my eyes I noticed a dark-haired girl in a track uniform snickering at me from her seat in the second row. I managed an awkward smile, but just then…

"Will!" a very excited sounding voice called out. The sound tugged at my ear and drew my gaze down the aisle to where Jeannine Fitsimmons, my best friend and business partner, was waiting for me. She stood out from the rest of the kids on the bus like a neon sign, sitting alone in her black leather jacket in a seat seven rows down, right next to the emergency exit as always. When I started making my way toward her, she began bouncing up and down in her seat, and she pounced when I was still two rows away.

"So, how did it go last night?" she gushed eagerly. "Did you find the monster? Did you…"

"Excuse me," I interrupted gruffly. "I seem to remember us saying something about keeping our…*business*…a secret."

Jeannine gasped, and clasped her hand to her mouth.

"Oh, right," she mumbled through her fingers, which were covered with black nail polish and several gothic skull rings. She sat back down and looked around as if to check whether or not anyone was listening, then motioned for me to join her. I walked over to her, but a large shoebox was filling up most of the seat.

"What's that?" I asked as Jeannine quickly picked up the box and sat it on her lap. I plopped down in the seat next to her, noticing as I did that she had added streaks of hot pink to her dyed black hair, which matched the pink paper clips she wore as earrings. That meant it must be Wednesday, because Wednesday is Jeannine's pink day.

"It's my diorama," she said excitedly. "Remember? The science project that's due today? Where's yours?"

I had been so focused on the case; I'd completely forgotten that our projects were due.

"I...I forgot mine," I mumbled.

"Will Allen!" she said in her high and mighty tone of voice. "I think you'd forget your head if it weren't attached."

I don't know about *you*, but that tone always gets under my skin.

"Well, if I can just *keep* it attached," I grumbled irritably, "then I won't have anything to worry about, will I?"

"You're going to lose points if you turn it in late," she chided. "So now maybe someone else can win the *outstanding science student* award for a change."

"You're just jealous!" I retorted crossly. "Anyway, with all the stuff your mom signs you up for, what with the music lessons, acting lessons, gymnastics classes, skating lessons and all, I doubt you had time to come up with anything very good."

"For your information," she said loftily, turning her nose upward, "she's also got me a science tutor. And my tutor says that this is the best diorama she's ever seen."

I just rolled my eyes.

"Well, that's some compliment," I grumbled. "Kind of like saying the best camel poop I ever smelled."

Jeannine just gave a *harrumph* and pulled her diorama away from me, like the cardboard box had been offended.

We didn't talk the rest of the way to school. Without Jeannine's usual blabber to listen to, the ride seemed much longer, so I just sat there thinking about what else might go wrong with my day. When we finally got to school though, everything went fine until Science Class, which I have just before lunch.

That's a good thing, because if it was after lunch, half the class would throw up from the formaldehyde smell in the room.

"Mr. Allen," called out Professor Munson, our science teacher. "Where is your science project?"

Now *I* was the one who felt like throwing up.

"I…ah, I forgot it, sir," I replied weakly.

"You forgot?" the professor said, with his bushy white eyebrows rising high upon his wrinkled, bald head. "I've been reminding the class every day for two weeks!"

"Yes sir. I'm sorry sir," was all I could say.

"Very well," he answered. He pulled his

horn-rimmed glasses off his face and straightened himself, then put the glasses back on and announced, "Ten points will be taken from your project grade…"

I sputtered.

"Ten points?"

"And ten more for each additional day it is late," he continued.

"But…but sir! I'm up for the science award! Ten points will…"

"I know you are up for the award, Mr. Allen. I am the one who nominated you, remember?" Professor Munson reminded. "But being up for the award does not excuse you from turning in assignments on time. Quite the contrary, it adds the responsibility of setting a good example for the rest of the class! Now, I will expect to see your project on my desk tomorrow. No excuses!"

"I don't believe...!" I started barking, but then I melted under the power of the professor's firm stare. "...Um, that is...*yes sir.*"

When I finally got to lunch, I was too bummed to eat. I sat poking at my macaroni & cheese, which looked suspiciously like one of the creatures that had lurked in the corner of my room the night Bigelow and I battled my monsters. I pulled out my MonsterScope, my special monster detecting magnifying glass, to check it out.

"So, are you going to eat that?" I heard Jeannine giggle from behind me. "Or is *it* going to eat *you*?"

I turned to look at her, checking her out with the MonsterScope as well.

Hey, you never know.

"Have you come to gloat?" I asked sharply.

"Oh, come on, Will," she said as she plopped down next to me. "Lighten up! You'll still win the award. You always do."

I just shrugged.

"Oh, come on!" she insisted, and stomped me on the foot. I hate when she does that, especially since she always wears steel-toed construction boots.

"Oooww! All right already!" I moaned.

Jeannine stared at me, but I just looked away.

"Anyway," she continued, "If you really want to get depressed, just check this out."

Jeannine opened her lunch bag and took out several zipper-sealed plastic bags.

"Alfalfa sprouts, green bean stew, and for dessert…"

"Sweet potato mousse," I grumbled without turning to look. "Give your mom credit…at least she's consistent."

And then we both stopped talking. Jeannine just kept glaring at me like she was expecting something.

"Well, are you going to tell me or what?" she finally blurted.

"Tell you what?" I growled back.

"What happened at Timmy's house last night?" Jeannine said impatiently. "Did you find the monster? Did you take care of it?"

I just kept looking away.

"Will," Jeannine said in a suddenly serious voice, "Did…did something go wrong? Did something bad happen?"

"No," I answered. "*Nothing* happened. That's the problem. And Timmy…"

Just as I spoke his name, Timmy appeared right in front of me. It kind of spooked me out at first. He just stood in front of me and growled.

"Stop bothering me!" he shouted.

I glared up at him.

"Um, define bothering," I suggested.

"I mean it!" he went on. "If you don't stop it I'll…"

"Stop what?" I yelled back heatedly. "I'm not doing anything."

"Stop it with the business cards! It's driving me crazy! They turn up everywhere now: in my backpack, in my pocket, my pillow. There was even one in my breakfast cereal this morning!"

Jeannine snorted, and milk came up through her nose. That made us both start laughing.

"Stop it!" Timmy yelled. "It's not funny!"

"Oh, I'm *so* sorry," I said scornfully. "But seeing as how you don't want my help anymore, there's not much I…"

"Doesn't want your help?" Jeannine injected. "Doesn't want to get rid of his…"

She looked around to be sure no one was listening.

"…his you know what?" she finished, turning back to Timmy and fixing him with an intent glare. "Is that true, Timmy?"

When Jeannine looked at him, Timmy's whole manner changed. He softened, looked down, and kicked at the floor.

"Yes, well...I...uh..."

"Timmy," Jeannine said softly, batting her eyelashes, "Didn't you ask me the other day to help you with your English homework? Do you want me to come tutor you?"

"Really?" Timmy said, his eyes suddenly wide. "Yeah! Can you come over this afternoon? I've got a big essay exam coming up..."

"Well, I would," she said slyly. "But I think I'd be too scared to come to a house that has a monster in it."

Timmy's face sank.

"Oh, right," he said as his body drooped.

"But maybe," Jeannine offered, "maybe if you and Will can work together to get rid of the monster, then it would be safe for me to come over."

"I, um...yeah. I guess that would be a good idea..." Timmy's expression grew twitchy and confused, like his brain was processing more thoughts than it could handle, which it probably was. He finally turned back to me and kind of mumbled, "Can you come over tonight, Will?"

Jeannine turned to me and smiled. I gave her a quick smirk back before I turned to Timmy and said, "I can't tonight. I have to finish my science project. Make it tomorrow instead."

"Okay then, tomorrow," Timmy replied. He

then looked back at Jeannine and waved.

"Bye then," he said.

"Bye, Timmy," she answered as he backed away smiling stupidly and tripped over a mop and bucket. Jeannine just giggled.

"Well, I guess you're back on the case," she said.

"But I'm not sure I *want* to be back on the case," I protested.

Jeannine coughed one of those *I forgot how to breathe* coughs.

"What?" she stammered. "Why not? Yesterday you were *thrilled* about becoming a monster detective."

I just looked away again.

"What's wrong, Will?" she asked urgently. "*Really*. You said I'd be your partner, remember? You have to tell me what's going on."

I slowly exhaled, and then looked back at her.

"Jeannine, did you ever get the feeling," I asked, "that everything is getting out of control?"

Jeannine's eyes lit up for a second, but then she put her hands together and frowned.

"Will," she said pointedly. "My mother tries to plan out my every waking moment. When do I ever even imagine things are *in* my control?"

I just looked at her. She tried not to let it show, but her face twitched a bit, like she was caught between feeling sad and angry.

"Sorry," I finally said. "I'm really sorry. All *my* mom does is ground me if I come home after 8:00."

"Don't worry about it," she said casually. "Now tell me what's wrong."

"I…" I began. "It's just that this monster detective stuff isn't like I thought it'd be. Last night, Timmy threw me out and told me I was useless…"

"Oh, don't let him get to you," Jeannine injected. "He's just…"

I cut her off.

"He was *right*," I told her. "I can't get rid of monsters, I can only try to shine light on them! Timmy's the one who has to face them down. And it doesn't exactly seem like he's eager to do that."

"Well, I don't know. Maybe now that he has the right incentive, he will be," Jeannine said. I didn't share her optimism.

"This bites!" I griped. "What good is it being a monster detective with no monster fighting powers of my own? That's like Spiderman without his webs, or Superman without his x-ray vision, or Plastic Man without his…well, his plastic."

"Actually, you're more like a Batman who's a bit too batty," Jeannine retorted. I glared at her.

"You're not helping," I snarled.

"Well then, *let* me help," she proposed, slapping her hands down in front of me. "Why don't you give me a crack at this?"

"What? What do you mean?" I sputtered.

"Let me help with the case," she suggested. "Tell me what's gone wrong."

I thought it over.

"Okay, look," I said. "Let me make this simple. To defeat monsters, we need light and bravery. *My* light, as it turns out, but *Timmy*'s bravery. The problem is, *I* have the bravery, but *Timmy* has the light."

Jeannine scratched her head. Whenever she does that, I pretty much know what she's going to say next.

"I don't get it," she finally blurted.

"Bigelow gave me a special flashlight. He calls it a RevealeR. The light it shines lets you see the hidden truth about your fears," I explained. "Timmy has to see his monsters for what they really are, and face them. But he won't do it."

"Can't you do it for him?"

"No. I can only shine the light. But I *have* no light."

"Why not?"

"Bigelow said that I need to understand the truth about the monsters before I can get the flashlight to work. You see, the RevealeR...well, it turns truth into light. That's what I have to use to fight the monsters."

"Can't you get rid of monsters without the flashlight?"

"No," I moaned. "I need the RevealeR to show Timmy the truth about the monsters and make them shrink. Without the RevealeR, we have no weapon to fight the monsters once we've found them. There's no other way to make the light."

Jeannine scratched her head.

"You could always just rub two sticks together." She suggested.

I scowled at her.

"You're not helping!" I barked. "The point is: I've got to figure out what that monster really is before I become its late-night snack."

Jeannine didn't have an answer for that, so we sat there quietly a while.

"So," she finally said. "We need to come up with a plan for what you're going to do."

"I've already *got* a plan," I answered. "I'm going to get Timmy to tell me more about the monster so that I can figure out what happened that caused it to come into our world, and then use my flashlight to show the truth about it to Timmy so that it will shrink down until it's not scary."

I smiled, certain that I had just come up with an infallible plan. Jeannine just stared at me.

"And how exactly," she asked, "are you going to get him to tell you *anything*?"

My smile crumbled like my mother's cookies {don't ask}.

"Um, I don't know," I said.

"Maybe for that," Jeannine suggested, "two heads would be better than one. Why don't I come along?"

I looked at her like she had just grown horns.

"Jeannine," I said crossly. "*I'm* the detective, remember? You've never even *seen* a monster. You wouldn't know what to do."

"Neither did you, until Bigelow showed you," she reminded. "And in case you hadn't noticed, *I* was the one who convinced Timmy to let you get back on the case. You may be good with monsters, Will, but I'm a lot better at dealing with people."

"But...But Jeannine," I protested. "You're a..."

A Girl. But I guessed that if I said that, she might get snippy.

"Um, that is, aren't you...you know..."

Afraid? Another sure kettle boiler.

"Ah, let me think it over," I finally concluded.

43

Chapter Five - Dodges

I had trouble focusing on my homework that night, and my science project, a giant model of how lasers work, was still dripping from the sloppy gobs of glue I had used to put it together when the phone rang.

"Have you thought it over, Will?" Jeannine asked without so much as a hello.

"Not now, Jeannine," I answered. "I'm trying to concentrate on my schoolwork."

"Schoolwork, huh? Isn't that the T.V. I hear?" she said.

"It's not *my* T.V," I told her. "It's coming in through the window. The neighbors always have the volume up too high."

"Harrumph!" she replied. "Just promise me that you *will* think about it?"

"I promise," I said. "Now will you let me get back to work?"

"Okay. Bye," she said, and hung up. I

slammed down the receiver.

Well actually, I didn't really slam it, because I already broke one phone last year and I didn't think my parents would believe me this time if I told them that one of the monsters did it. But I definitely *felt* like slamming something. The truth was that I *had* been thinking about it, and there was no way I saw anything good coming from Jeannine being in that room with me, Timmy, and the monsters. How could I protect her from being eaten alive, when I wasn't even sure I could protect myself?

Of course, she couldn't just let it go.

"So, have you thought it over, Will?" was how she greeted me on the school bus the following morning.

"*Have you thought it over, Will*?" quickly became the phrase of the day. I heard it in class, at lunch, and on the bus ride home. Ten minutes after I came in the door, the phone rang.

"Have you thought it over, Will?" Jeannine said.

I hung up the phone. For the rest of the afternoon, every time my mother called out to me to say I had a phone call, which was about every five minutes, I told her I had to go to the bathroom.

Finally, evening came, and I prepared to set out for Timmy's house. Then the phone rang one more time.

"Will," my mother called out. "It's for you. Jeannine is on the phone. Would you please take it this time?"

"Sorry, mom," I said, quickly throwing on my coat and hat. "I've got to run over to Timmy's house. Tell her I'll call her back."

"Do you think you can make it all the way there without stopping?" my mother said tartly. "Or should I send you with a port-a-potty?"

"I think I can hold it," I said dryly as I headed for the door.

"I hope they have a lot of toilet tissue in that house," she muttered as she turned away.

"Well," Timmy's mom said as she let me in. "With all this tutoring, I certainly expect to see a big improvement in Timmy's math grade this term."

"Uh, right," I answered, thinking as I did that I wanted to be nowhere near this house when the next report card showed up. But then, I would have to survive a battle with terrifying monsters before worrying about that.

That's the great thing about this job: it helps put everything else in perspective.

Timmy came into the foyer from his kitchen. He quickly hid something behind his back when his mother spotted him.

"Oh, hi Will," he said nervously. "Well, come on, we've got a lot of work to do."

And then he grabbed my arm again and began

tugging.

"Just a minute, young man," his mother stopped him. "What's that behind your back?"

Timmy tried to turn away from her, but his mom reached around behind his back and pulled from his hand a bag of chocolate bars.

"Sneaking food up to your room again?" she scolded. "How many times have I told you…"

"It's for Will," Timmy said. "He said that he needs lots of chocolate to snack on when he's…ah, *tutoring*."

Timmy's mother looked at me accusingly.

"Oh, really?" she scoffed.

"I, ah…It helps me think," I offered. She obviously wasn't buying it, because the scowl lines began growing deep on her face again.

"You're here to study, not have a party," she said sternly. Then she took the bag and ushered us out of the foyer to the stairs.

"Oh, and Timmy, you left the phone off the hook. *Again*!"

"Right, mom," Timmy said mechanically. "Sorry, mom."

He said no more, but when we got to the top of the stairs, he turned to me and smiled as he pulled several chocolate bars out of his pockets.

"I'm way ahead of her," he said smugly.

When Timmy opened the door to his room, I couldn't believe my eyes.

"What…what happened here? Did a monster do this?" I asked, staring at the frenzied mess the room had become. Clothes and toys were everywhere, the mattress was off the bed and propped up horizontally, with stacks of books piled around the sides to form a makeshift bunker. Inside the bunker were a net, baseballs, a bat, a hockey stick, and a football helmet. And on the floor in the center of the room was a plate, with the table that had Timmy's phone on it standing nearby. Timmy placed the chocolate down in the middle of the plate.

"It's the bait," Timmy explained. "I hope this one works."

"You're trying to trap it?" I asked.

Timmy nodded.

"I tried yesterday, too," he explained. "I told my mom I needed an extra peanut butter and jelly sandwich for lunch, but she gave me liverwurst! Even monsters won't eat liverwurst!"

"Timmy," I said exasperatedly. "It won't work. I know from experience, it won't work."

"You've tried trapping monsters?" he asked.

I nodded.

"With a brownie ice cream sundae," I told him.

"And it didn't work?" He seemed shocked.

"No," I said flatly. "Monsters feed off of our fears. And I'm sure you've been giving them a steady diet of that."

"Why didn't you tell me that before?" Timmy asked crossly.

Because I didn't know, I thought. But I wasn't telling Timmy that.

"Well, maybe this time you'll keep me around long enough to tell you what you need to know." I answered instead. Timmy gave me a sheepish look.

"Look, I'm sorry about kicking you out the other night…"

"Never mind!" I said irritably. "Let's just clear some room in this mess so I can get to work. With my luck, I'll trip over one of these toys in the dark and break my neck."

I didn't say, *before the monsters have a chance to do it for me*. But I was thinking it.

I got down and began sweeping the toys and books into piles at the side of the room. I looked back, expecting to see Timmy doing the same, but he was in his bunker, putting on the football helmet.

"What are you doing?" I asked angrily.

"Putting on protection," he answered. "You never know when a monster might try to pierce your skull and suck out your brains."

"Oh, you don't know what you're talking about," I grumbled. But I secretly began wishing that I had brought a helmet too.

"All right," I announced. "That's good enough. Let's get started."

I walked over to the light switch.

"Are you ready?" I asked as I held my hand to the switch. Timmy, crouching in his bunker with his helmet drooping in front of his eyes and a hockey stick held tightly with both hands, nodded. I flicked the switch. The room went dark, and that eerie blue glow that had filled it two nights before returned. I flicked the switch on my flashlight. It flickered a bit, and then a steady stream of light came out, but it was extremely dim, and strangely greenish.

"It looks like you need new batteries," Timmy said.

"It doesn't take batteries," I answered. "It's…uh, rechargeable."

"And you didn't charge it before coming?" Timmy complained.

"It's charged!" I insisted. "It just needs time

to warm up."

"Well it better warm up fast!" Timmy said urgently. His hands were starting to shake. "It won't be long before..."

All of a sudden, there was a knocking sound. It started softly, but then grew louder, echoing throughout the room. I swung my flashlight around in every direction to try and spot where it was coming from.

"It's here!" Timmy bellowed. "It's here! Turn on the light! See if it ate the chocolate!"

"I told you, it doesn't want chocolate! Now be quiet!" I ordered.

The knocking sound continued, but my light still wasn't spying anything. Something was very wrong.

Just then, the door to the room began shaking

violently. Timmy hid behind me while I turned the beam of my RevealeR to the door and shined my light on it, but it revealed nothing at all. Then the shaking stopped, and we both breathed a small sigh of relief.

Suddenly, there was a loud bang, and the door shook once more. Timmy fell back and whimpered, and then there was another loud bang and the door exploded open.

Chapter Six - Collaborations

Into the doorway stepped a dark silhouette. Its shape was very much like a pterodactyl.

"Stupid door!" the figure in the shadows muttered. "…Should have had that fixed ages ago…"

"Look out!" Timmy cried out. "It's the monster!"

"Relax," I said, lowering my flashlight. "It's just your mom."

"Same thing," Timmy muttered.

"What's going on in here?" Timmy's mother called to us as she pushed her way into the room. "How can you study math in a pitch-black room?"

Timmy and I looked at each other.

"Um, we were taking a break," I stuttered quickly, hiding my flashlight in my back pocket while Timmy kicked the plate of chocolate bars under his bed. "There were some fireflies outside, and we turned out the light so we could..."

"What are you doing, checking up on me?" Timmy spouted angrily.

"No," his mother said firmly. "I've been knocking on your door to tell you that you have another guest."

"Another guest?" Timmy spat. "Who?"

And from behind Timmy's mother, in walked Jeannine.

"Jeannine?" I sputtered. "I thought I told you…"

"I thought it over about you thinking it over," she said firmly. "And then I decided that I was done thinking about whether I should let you go on thinking about it. So, here I am."

After unraveling what she had just said, I wasn't quite sure whether I admired her gumption or hated it. But I was sure that there wasn't much I could do about it either way.

"What's with the dress?" I grumbled with a sour look on my face. "Since when do you wear…*flowery* stuff?"

Jeannine just smirked and glanced over at Timmy, but before she could speak…

"What's been going on in here?" Timmy's mother spouted as she looked around the room. The sight of that terrible mess seemed to horrify her more than any giant flying shark ever could. "Have you two been fighting?"

"No!" Timmy answered crossly.

"Then why is everything strewn all over the

room like this? And why are you wearing your father's old football helmet?"

She reached over and pulled the helmet off the top of his head.

"Honestly!" she grumbled. "I don't see how you could need this to study math!"

"Ooowww! But mom," Timmy protested. "I need to protect myself from the…you know…"

"Enough of this nonsense!" his mother declared. "I want this room cleaned up immediately, young man!"

Timmy's head slumped, but then he caught sight of Jeannine. She was pointedly looking away from him with an embarrassed expression on her face, and Timmy's posture suddenly stiffened.

"It's *my* room!" Timmy challenged defiantly. "If I don't mind the mess, neither should you!"

His mother gave Timmy a withering look.

"You'll clean this room right now or I'll give you something to *really* be scared of!" she declared, and then she stormed out of the room. Jeannine and I just stood there, totally speechless.

"Still think she's not a monster?" Timmy asked.

"Well," Jeannine responded. "I'd certainly be terrified if that was hiding under *my* bed."

"Well, there's nothing I can do," I added glumly. "I'm a detective, not a social worker. Come on, let's get back to it."

"Okay, let's," Jeannine agreed. Timmy and I just stared at her.

"Jeannine…" I said.

"I'm a part of the team," she said with her *and that's final* tone of voice. "I'm staying."

"Jeannine," I said. "You can't. You don't have any of the…*detective* stuff you need."

"Like what?" she asked huffily.

"Well, for one thing, you would need a…" I began saying, but then a strange thing happened. When I reached into my back pocket to take out my special flashlight, I found *two* there. The first was my RevealeR, the red one that Bigelow had given me, but there was another one that was yellow and decorated all over with little white daisies. Naturally, I handed Jeannine the yellow one.

"I think this must be for you," I said.

You'd think that she'd be thrilled to have her own RevealeR, but she looked at it suspiciously.

"Yours is bigger," she complained.

Sometimes she can be such a pain.

"Bigelow said size doesn't matter," I barked.

"Fine," she answered. "Then you won't mind if I get the bigger one."

"This one is mine," I hissed. "It's the one Bigelow gave me. This new one is obviously for a girl, I mean, just look at it. It has *daisies*!"

Jeannine didn't answer, she just stomped on my foot. I growled at her, but just then, Timmy spoke up.

"Excuse me, but who is Bigelow?"

"Never mind," I answered grumpily.

"I still need a magnifying glass," Jeannine pointed out.

"A *MonsterScope*," I corrected.

"Whatever!" Jeannine growled. "The point is, I need one!"

I reached into my other pocket for my MonsterScope, but there was still just one. I held it up.

"Just one," I showed her. "Sorry."

"Well then, what do I use?" she complained.

"I don't know. Maybe you can just use your glasses."

Did I mention before that Jeannine wears glasses?

I guess it never came up. She usually only wears them for reading, because she thinks they make her look dorky. Anyway, she took them out of her pocket, studied them a bit, and then put them on, squinting strangely.

She *did* look dorky.

"But, how do I turn them on?" she asked.

"Hey!" Timmy called out. "What about me? Don't I get some kind of monster fighting ray gun or something?"

Jeannine and I just turned and stared at him, Jeannine with that weird squinty look, and me with my magnifying glass in front of my eye like a giant monocle.

"Just leave this to the professionals," I told him.

"Harrumph!" Timmy growled irritably. He pulled the plate of chocolate out from under the bed, put it back in the center of the room, and then he climbed over one of the stacks of books and sat behind the propped up mattress.

"Wait a minute," I said. "Where are you going?"

"Into my fort, where it's safe," he answered.

I just glared at him.

"Then how do you expect to find the monsters?"

"*You're* the detective," he spat. "Detect something!"

I looked at Jeannine, but she just shrugged.

"Fine!" I said impatiently. "We'll try it your way. Let's get started then."

And I walked over and turned out the light, then Jeannine and I joined Timmy behind his makeshift barricades.

An hour later, we were still sitting there, bored, and growing restless.

"There!" Timmy cried out. "Something is moving over there! Is that it?"

I lifted my MonsterScope looked through the glass at where he pointed. What looked like waves of creepy black fingers were crawling across the floor, drifting back and forth in time with the blowing winds outside.

"No," I said plainly. "Those are just shadows from the tree outside."

"What about that over there?" he swiftly added. "Those clumps under my desk. Are those, like... monster droppings or something?"

I bent down and checked it out.

"No, those are dust bunnies," I said dejectedly.

"This is boring," Jeannine complained.

"You wanted to be a detective," I pointed out. "This is what it's like."

"But can't we *do* something?" she whined.

"Not while we're hiding back here, no."

Timmy scowled.

"What's wrong with these stupid monsters?" he complained. "Why won't they eat this stuff?"

"I told you before," I groused. I was feeling rather ornery at this point. "This isn't what they want. The only bait that will work is *you*."

"Thanks *so* much," Timmy replied. "But it's not my goal in life to be a monster's happy meal!"

"More like an *un*happy meal," Jeannine grumbled.

"What?" he turned to her. "What's that?"

"Never mind!" I snapped. "You know, I'm not interested in being monster chow either! But I'm here!" Then I turned and pointed at Jeannine.

"We *both* came here to help you! Both of us are here to fight monsters for you! But we have to do this my way. Now are you ready to face this monster or not?"

Timmy looked at me, and then over a Jeannine, who stood firm. Then he looked down.

"Even a *girl*," he mumbled, "Even a girl is braver than me."

Timmy squirmed and kicked at the ground, but wouldn't look up at us. He seemed to be ashamed that Jeannine was prepared to face the danger that he shied away from.

*Okay, maybe something good **can** come from having her around*, I thought.

"All right," Timmy finally said. "What should I do?"

"For a start," I instructed, "let's all come out of hiding."

I stepped out from behind the barricades and walked to the center of the room. As I turned and looked back, Jeannine stood and climbed over a pile of books and joined me. Timmy hesitated, scanning the room nervously, but when nothing jumped out at us he breathed a heavy sigh, held his breath, and strode gingerly out of his place of safety and into the eerie darkness that spread before us all.

Chapter Seven ~ Courtesies

Timmy kept glancing around nervously, twitching his head to the sound of every rustle of the leaves or chirping of crickets that drifted in through the stillness all around us. With every shudder and tremble that ran up Timmy's spine, the shadows around us seemed to grow deeper and darker.

"Well, now what?" Timmy blurted.

"Don't worry," I told him. "I have a plan."

I picked up the plate of chocolate bars and put them on the desk.

"Now," I said firmly, "we set our trap with the only thing that works: live bait." Then I pulled a chair into the center of the room.

"Sit down," I instructed.

"Don't mind if I do," Jeannine said casually as she took off her glasses and slid them into her pocket, then plopped down into the chair. "That floor was very uncomfortable…"

"Not you!" I growled. "Timmy! Timmy has to sit there!"

"Oh, right," she said sheepishly, jumping up at once.

"But…but my dad says it's not polite for a gentleman to take a lady's seat…" Timmy protested.

"Down!" I ordered.

"Humph! Some people have no manners," Timmy grumbled as he sat himself in the chair. His eyes immediately began darting around anxiously, and the room grew darker still. I flicked the switch on my flashlight, which came on, but still with only that very dim, greenish light.

"I told you that you should have charged that thing!" Timmy said nervously.

"Oh, shut up!" I barked. "Now stop whining and tell us what it is you're so scared of."

"I'm scared of the monsters, you idiot!" Timmy shouted. "I'm scared of…"

Just then, a loud ringing sound began echoing all through the room. Timmy froze like a stone, while I immediately walked over and checked out the phone on the small table with my MonsterScope. But there were no glowing spots on it this time. And there was no ring there either. It was just a plain old telephone.

"But…but that can't be…" I muttered. "Something was *there* last time. I know it was!"

So I looked closer, searching for any signs of a monster, but nothing appeared in the sight of my scope. But as I leaned in further, I noticed something. Something important.

The receiver was slightly ajar. The phone had been left off the hook.

Timmy, you left the phone off the hook. Again. His mother had said that. Timmy must have been leaving the phone off the hook a lot. I looked over at him as he sat in the center of the room, and saw him staring nervously back.

"I wonder…" I muttered softly, and then I lifted the receiver and placed it properly on the base of the phone. Timmy's eyes grew wide, and his teeth began chattering.

"S-stop…stop messing with my stuff!" he sputtered.

Without a word, I put the receiver back the way it was. Instantly Timmy's eyes relaxed, and he exhaled deeply. But then the ringing continued, and he stiffened again.

"He…he's been doing it on *purpose*," I whispered to myself.

As that thought filled my brain, the beam of light from my flashlight grew brighter, though overall it still remained rather dim.

"Timmy," I asked, "who have you been getting phone calls from?"

"No one!" he screeched. "I don't know what you're talking about!"

"Then why are you so afraid of the phone ringing?"

"I'm not! I…I…"

But just as suddenly as it began, the ringing stopped. I shined my flashlight all around, but still saw no signs of the monster. Timmy sighed with relief, but then…

" I ' M...SORRY... " spoke a loud, high-pitched, echoing voice. "I'M...SORRY...BUT..."

"NO!" Timmy cried out. "No! Go away!"

And he jumped out of the chair and dashed back to his fortress, but he tripped over one of the books in the dark and went sprawling. He knocked over one of the piles of books and crashed into his dresser, knocking down a heavy bookend that crashed to the floor mere inches from his head.

"I'M...SORRY," the voice followed him. "I'M SORRY, BUT...HE CAN'T..."

"No!" Timmy screamed from the floor as he

crawled behind the mattress. "Leave me alone!"

"I'M SORRY, BUT HE...CAN'T...COME...TO THE PHONE."

"Nooooooo!" Timmy cried.

I just stared at him.

"What is it?" I asked. "What voice is that?"

"Never mind what it is!" he shouted. "Just get rid of it!"

"It doesn't work that way," I told him. "You have to do what I tell you."

"I tried doing what you told me!" Timmy shouted. "And it nearly killed me!"

"You big baby!" I yelled. "You're not helping!"

"Neither are *you*," I was told. I just froze, because the scolding hadn't come from Timmy. It was Jeannine.

"What? What are you saying?" I asked her angrily.

"I'm saying that you have the people skills of a gnat," she retorted.

"Well, don't sugar-coat it, Jeannine. Say what you really think!"

"I'm saying you could use a little tact," she said pointedly.

"And some manners!" Timmy added.

I bristled.

"I don't need this!" I shouted.

"Yes you do," she insisted. "Have you gotten Timmy to tell you what we need to know?"

I looked at my flashlight. It was still dim.

"No," I answered.

"Then let me try."

I looked at Timmy, cowering behind his mattress, and decided to give in.

Yes, I really *do* hate doing that.

"All right," I mumbled grudgingly. I put my RevealeR back in my pocket and stepped aside.

Jeannine walked over to Timmy, who was crouched and shivering. She knelt down and put her hand on his shoulder.

"I'M SORRY, BUT HE... CAN'T... COME... TO... THE PHONE," the monster voice called out.

Timmy and Jeannine shuddered together, and I wondered why the voice affected both of them like that, but not me.

"Timmy," Jeannine said softly. "I understand. You don't have to explain. I feel it too."

"You do?" I sputtered. "Well then..."

"Be quiet, Will!" she ordered, then turned back to Timmy, who looked up at her timidly.

"Don't be mad at Will," she told him. "It's not the same for him. He just doesn't know what it's like."

I become indignant.

"What are you talking about?"

"Shut up, Will!" they said together. I just folded my arms.

"Fine!" I grumbled, and began drumming my fingers.

"Timmy," Jeannine said softly. "I *know* now what the monster is. But *where* is it, Timmy? I need for you to tell me."

Timmy looked at her and melted.

"Over there," he stuttered, pointing with a shaking hand. "It's in the top left drawer of my desk."

Jeannine smiled gently, and patted his shoulder. Then she got up and walked to the desk.

I was flabbergasted.

"You *knew*?" I bellowed at him. "You knew all along where it was?!"

But Timmy said nothing: he was staring fixedly at Jeannine as she approached the desk. She hesitated briefly in front of it, but then took hold of the drawer and opened it in one swift motion. A bright golden glow erupted from the drawer.

"I'M SORRY, BUT HE...CAN'T...COME...TO THE PHONE," cried out the voice of the monster, louder than ever before. The drawer shook violently as the monster-voice erupted, but then was still.

"Jeannine!" I called out excitedly as I stepped up to examine the drawer with my MonsterScope. "You did it! You uncovered the monster! Good work!"

But Jeannine didn't seem too pleased with her success.

"I…" she stuttered, stumbling back from the desk. "I…have to go to the bathroom."

"Not now, Jeannine!" I said, but she grabbed my shirt and tugged hard.

"I really have to go…" she insisted.

I looked hard at her. Utter terror filled her eyes.

"Jeannine, it's just a little ring…" I protested.

"I have to go *now*!" she screeched, and then turned and ran for the door.

"You're running away? From a little ring?"

But she didn't stop. She opened the door, yet the room remained black.

"You...you..." I sputtered. "You're such a *girl!*"

But she just ran out, and the door closed behind her.

Chapter Eight - Illuminations

I was still staring at the door in frozen disbelief when Timmy grabbed my sleeve and tugged hard.

"Why did you do that?" Timmy yelled. "You scared her away!"

I couldn't believe what I was hearing.

"*I* scared her?" I yelled back. "It wasn't me, it was this stupid little…"

I stopped yelling, because when I turned back to the desk, I saw the golden ring hovering in mid-air just inside the open drawer. Its eerie kaleidoscopic glow was strong and bright now even without using the MonsterScope. As I watched, it floated up out of the drawer and drifted toward us, slowly rotating like a planet in space. The center of the ring shimmered like a disco ball, and beams of light projected from it in every direction. The rays struck the walls, creating a sea of hazy blotches that danced around the room. As they moved, trails of very soft, distant whispers followed. I stared hard at the projected sparkles on the wall, but they were just blurs of light and darkness. At least, they were to me.

"Noooo!" Timmy cried. "Look what you've done! Keep back!"

"Keep *what* back?" I asked. "It's just…"

But again I stopped short. As I spun around, I caught sight of one of the blurs on the wall, and saw that it was…well, *growing*. The blur pulsed and throbbed as it drifted across the wall, becoming larger and brighter. It kept growing until it was an oblong blob about as tall as Timmy and twice as wide. The pulsing continued, and the blob began to swell, filling out like an inflating balloon. As we stared, speechless and horrified, the blob began thrusting in our direction, and finally pulled itself *right off the wall*. It kept coming toward us, growing ever larger as it approached.

"Is…is   that…the   monster?"   Timmy whimpered.

"Well, it's no dust bunny," I retorted.

"What do I do now?" he wailed.

"Face it!" I commanded. "Be brave and stand up to it!"

"Are you crazy!? It probably has oozing tentacles that paralyze you with just a touch!"

"Good!" I shouted. "It can start with your mouth!"

Then I shoved him toward the monster. He looked up at it and stiffened. Instead of breathing, he made a sound like a squeaky wheel when he tried to inhale. The monster drew in close and rose high above him as Timmy cowered helplessly.

"Well," I said quietly, steeling myself as I pulled my flashlight back out of my pocket, "It looks like it's time to be a hero." I looked down at my RevealeR and flicked the switch.

"Come *on*," I growled nervously. "I need some light...*now*!" But the light that erupted from my RevealeR was still weak and feeble. I looked back at Timmy as the glowing blob began to envelop him. The light seemed to be wrapping itself around him, as if it was about to swallow him whole.

"Please!" he cried. "Please...*do* something!"

I bit my lip.

"Here goes nothing," I whispered.

I dove right between the glowing blob and Timmy, and shined the sparse light of my flashlight squarely at the monster. A horrible moaning wail erupted from the blob and echoed loudly through the room. The glow grew even brighter. and I felt myself being invisibly sucked in toward the monster.

"I'm being pulled in!" I shouted as I struggled to stay back. I reached out blindly for something to grab on to, and my hand found Timmy's arm.

"I...I've got you!" Timmy cried out as he grasped tightly on to my sleeve. At that very moment, the light from my RevealeR flared, and the beam turned bluish. The glimmering blob throbbed, but then the pulsing of its light died and the glow began to fade. The pull weakened, and I drew back, and squinted hard.

"There...there's something *in* there..." I called out. "There's something inside the glowing blob!"

And as the glow surrounding it faded, the form within grew apparent.

"D...Daddy?" Timmy mumbled. His hand dropped from my sleeve, and the light from my RevealeR faded.

"Your dad?" I said. "What is it about fathers? *My* monster was my dad too."

But Timmy didn't answer. Neither did the monster that looked like his father. I shined my RevealeR in his face, but it had no effect on him: he just turned and walked casually toward the phone by the closet door.

"It was *him*," I guessed. "He must have been the one that left the monster prints on the phone."

I turned back to Timmy, who was staring at the monster with his mouth hanging open. He was drooling onto his chin, but somehow it seemed like a bad time for me to point that out.

"Timmy!" I shouted, shaking him to get his attention. "What does he do? What does your dad say on the phone that scares you so much?"

"What?" he replied dazedly. "I...I don't know what you're talking about."

"You don't...?" But then I froze. Timmy's father-monster had reached the table upon which the phone sat, but when he reached down to pick up the receiver, the loud, shrieking voice echoed through the room again.

"**No!**" it wailed. "**Mine!**"

"Wha..." I muttered. "Who...?"

Suddenly, the air around us grew bright with streaks of orange and red. I looked back, and the golden ring, which still hovered near the desk, was enflamed with a burning halo, its golden glow replaced by crimson fires. The sparkling rays that erupted from its center turned into shooting flames, and spears of fire began to strike all around us.

"Run!" Timmy cried as he stumbled back. "Head for the fort!"

"No!" I shouted, grabbing him by the shirt and pulling him back. "You have to stand up to it..."

At just that moment, I screamed as a burst of flame shot through the air and scorched my shoulder, burning a huge, searing hole in my jacket. I looked down at my smoldering coat, and then up at Timmy, who was still tangled in my grasp. We stared blankly at each other for a second.

"Um, new plan," I muttered as more jets of fire shot out at us. *Run for your life*!!!"

Timmy and I dove for cover just as flames engulfed the spot where we had been standing. We positioned ourselves behind the upright mattress, then turned back to see what was happening. As we stared in rapt horror, Timmy's father was blasted head-on by a spear of fire. He stumbled, and then staggered blindly backward. When he turned around to face us, we both recoiled in terror.

"Oh my god..." Timmy mumbled. "Oh, no! *Daddyyyyy*!"

For the figure before us no longer bore a face, just a gaping, charred hole that stretched from ear to ear. An awful green slime began slowly seeping from the ragged flesh.

"I think I'm going to puke," I moaned.

But as if that wasn't enough to send us running for the nearest bathroom, things got even worse. A set of giant fangs suddenly grew out of that oozing hole, and then the monster straightened up, and began taking stumbling steps in our direction. Timmy cowered and backed away, but I held my ground, and turned my flashlight on the creature, pointing its weak beam as steadily as my shaking hands would allow.

But the monster kept growing.

"I'M SORRY, BUT HE CAN'T COME TO THE PHONE AT THE MOMENT," spoke the terrible, shrieking voice, which seemed to come from all around us.

"Timmy!" I called back without looking, keeping my eyes and my light fixed squarely on the monster in front of me, whose horrible, slimy fangs kept growing nearer. "Timmy, that voice…it's not coming from this monster! Whose voice is that, Timmy? If it's not your dad, whose voice is it?"

"**Put him on the phone**!" Timmy's voice echoed through the room. "**Put him on right now**!"

"Put him on the phone?" I asked puzzledly, turning quickly to look at Timmy. "What does…"

But when I saw Timmy's face, it was frozen in a terrified whimper. When I looked at him, he began shaking his head back and forth and silently mouthed the words, "No, no, no…"

"That voice…" I realized, "That was your voice, Timmy. But it *wasn't* you, was it?"

Timmy shook his head.

"But if the voice didn't come from you," I reasoned, "and it didn't come from me, then…"

As I spoke, the light from my RevealeR grew just a bit stronger. The monster in front of me, with fangs that now stretched from the top of its burned-out head to its blackened, scorched chin, staggered a moment, but then kept advancing. I pointed my RevealeR right at the slimy hole that used to be its face, but it did not shrink, or slow down. I looked down at my RevealeR, and then back up at the slimy mess.

"You…" I said to the monster, "You're not the one…"

Then I looked over at the ring, which continued to hover and shoot fiery rays from across the room. I hesitated a moment, but then I turned my RevealeR from the monster in front of me and pointed it at the ring. It instantly stopped shooting flames and began shaking, and then…

"**Put him on**!" the echoing voice that sounded like Timmy repeated as the ring vibrated in tune with the voice. "**You put him on the phone! I know he's there**!"

The real Timmy shivered.

"Daddy, no," he whimpered to himself. "Daddy, please come home and save me."

That was when it hit me.

"Timmy…your father, he...he doesn't live here anymore, does he?'

"He does!" the real Timmy shouted. "He's just working late! He'll be coming home!"

I just looked at him.

"Are your parents...getting divorced?" I asked in as gentle a tone as I could.

I guess Jeannine was right about me not being very tactful, because that made Timmy lose it.

"No!" he screeched, grabbing me with both hands. "No they're just...sorting things out, that's all. My dad will come home soon! He promised!"

And then Timmy did the worst thing he could

possibly do. He started crying.

Guys, back me up on this.

Well, with Timmy clinging to my shirt, crying, my flashlight still dim, and a slimy monster with giant fangs about to devour us alive, I was pretty much bummed out. I tried pointing my RevealeR at the monster again, but the beam had no effect.

"Jeannine," I called out weakly. "This would be a real good time to rub two sticks together."

The monster finally reached the mattress that stood between us and in one swift motion flung it aside like my dad tossing his laundry when he's searching for a clean set of socks. It rose above us, with those hideous fangs dripping, and prepared to strike.

At that very moment, the door to Timmy's room burst open, and in strode Jeannine, flashlight in hand.

"Take this, you creep!" she bellowed as she flicked the switch and shined her light on the beast. Its slightly pinkish beam was bright and strong, and the monster screeched, and fell back. It cowered, and started flailing its arms wildly as if to fight off the beam. I stepped over to Jeannine.

"Took your sweet time about it, didn't you?" I complained.

"I wasn't sure you really needed me," she said casually.

"Drama Queen," I grumbled as I turned back to the monster, which was shrieking, and began shaking violently.

"Look," Timmy said. "It…it…"

"It's shrinking," I confirmed.

"Hold this!" Jeannine instructed as she tried forcing her flashlight into my hand.

"What? Why?" I protested.

"Just hold it!" she insisted as she shoved it into my fingers, and then hurried over to Timmy. As her RevealeR transferred from her hand to mine, its light immediately began to dim.

"Um, I think it likes you better," I mumbled as the light faded. Darkness closed in on us, and the monster began to grow again. It rose and turned toward us.

"Jeannine, we have a problem!" I called out. But Jeannine just ignored me. She always picks the worst times to do that.

"Timmy!" she said as she bent down to him.

"Timmy, everything will be okay. My mom and dad got divorced too."

"No!" he cried. "My mom and dad are not..."

"Timmy, I was scared too. But you know what? Things are much better now. My mom and dad are both happier. And now I don't hear them yelling at each other all the time."

That was when I finally understood what had happened earlier.

"Jeannine," I said. "You couldn't stand looking at the monster because it was *your* monster too, wasn't it?"

She just nodded.

"Um, sorry about calling you a...you know, a *girl,*" I said.

"Later," she hissed, and turned back to Timmy, who still cowered, sobbing. "Timmy, things are much better now. Even though my dad's not living with me anymore, I know he still loves me."

"No!" Timmy cried. "No, it's all a lie! He said he'd always be here when I need him. Well, I need him *now*! So where is he?"

At that, Jeannine fell back.

"I...I   don't   know..."   she   said. "Maybe…maybe he…"

"No! It's just a lie!" Timmy insisted. "He's never there for me! And I bet *your* dad is never there for you either!"

"N-no…it's not true," Jeannine mumbled, but

then she fell into a sitting position and looked up, her eyes growing damp and glassy. The monster seemed to sense their growing despair, and began staggering toward them, groping frantically in their direction like someone on a diet reaching desperately for a hot fudge sundae.

"No!" I cried out, as I leapt over to Timmy and Jeannine and jumped in front of the monster. "Leave her alone!" I shined both RevealeRs on the monster, but the light did not slow it down. Jeannine grabbed a hold of Timmy's sleeve as the monster drew ever closer.

If ever I needed to do some quick thinking, this was the time.

No, he can't come to the phone at the moment? Why was that so terrifying? Did that mean something terrible had happened, and Timmy couldn't reach his dad for help?

"No," I thought out loud. "Then why would Timmy purposely leave phones off the hook?" I looked at Timmy and Jeannine, cowering as the monster grew gigantic and rose above us.

"He doesn't *want* to reach his dad," I realized. "He doesn't want to hear..."

No, he can't come to the phone at the moment. But maybe Timmy hadn't been calling his dad's *office...*

"Timmy, does your dad have...a girlfriend?"

"Nooooooo!" he wailed. "No, he's going to come home! He's going to come save me from the monster!"

My flashlight suddenly lit like fire, and Jeannine's, which was still in my other hand, grew bright again too. But before I could move, the monster's flailing arms swooped in and grabbed me, pinning my arms to my sides, and then it began lifting me toward its terrible fangs.

"Will! Oh, no!" Jeannine cried. "You…you stop that, you stupid monster! Leave him alone! Are you listening to me? I said leave him alone!"

Leave it to Jeannine to think she could defeat a monster by nagging it to death.

As for me, I knew that there was no time for asking any more questions. I squirmed and tugged as the monster drew me in close, and managed to pull one arm free.

"I think I understand now," I said as I stared into that slimy maw, "So, take this!" And I turned the beam from my flashlight back onto the monster.

"Come on!" I urged, shaking my RevealeR desperately. "I need you to work…*NOW*!"

Only nothing happened. The monster's face turned into a ghastly hair to chin, ear to ear grin, as it drew me toward its mouth. I was so close that the slime from its teeth dripped on my face…

Now I don't mind telling you, my whole body was shaking like our car did the day my dad poured brake fluid where the oil was supposed to go. But at just that moment, I heard Bigelow's voice in the back of my brain.

To defeat monsters, we must first master our fears, he had told me. *Begin by taking control of your breathing.*

My breaths were coming in fits and gasps, but I was too focused on keeping my head from becoming the monster's chew toy to pay much attention to that.

Calm your breathing, and you will calm your mind. Then you can see past the fear, Bigelow had said.

"Calm my breathing," I gasped to myself. "I'll try."

So even as I struggled to keep the monster from chowing down on my face, I tried to focus on my breathing. I inhaled as deeply and slowly as I could, and as my breaths grew steadier, it was like a fog began to lift from my brain. Unfortunately, my brain was very near to entering the monster's throat.

Focus, I thought to myself. *See past the fear.*

I forced down another deep, steady breath, and at that very moment, the light from my flashlight flared, and the monster's entire form started shaking and writhing. Its grin faded, turning to a scowl of rage. I pointed the light right into the monster's slimy jaws, and it shrieked with fury. Then, incredibly, that horrible face melted, and began to change. The monster's grip on me began to weaken, and I squirmed to slip free.

"Timmy," I called out as I dropped back to the floor. "This will hurt, but you've got to face the monster. If you don't, it will never leave you."

"Noooooooo!" he cried. "After what it almost did to *you*? I can't!"

"Timmy," Jeannine said. "I couldn't look at it either. But maybe we can do it together! We can be braver together!"

And she tugged on Timmy's arm, making him rise, reluctantly, to his feet.

"Come on!" she prodded. "We can do it."

She gave him a gentle nudge, urging him to look.

"Hey!" I complained as I stepped over beside her and handed her back her flashlight. "How come he gets a little nudge, and I always get my foot stomped on?"

She just stomped my foot again.

"Owww!" I bellowed as I hopped in pain.

Then Jeannine looked back at Timmy, nodded, and together they looked up at the monster.

"There!" Jeannine said encouragingly. "That's not so bad!"

"It…it's horrible…" Timmy said weakly, shielding his eyes as though he were looking into the sun.

"It *is* horrible," I agreed, as I straightened up and turned to face that grotesque, slimy monster again. "But that's not the one."

"Not…the one?" Timmy mumbled.

"Not the true monster," I answered. "I understand that now."

And then I lifted my RevealeR and pointed its beam back at the monster. The light was strong, much brighter than it had been before, and when it hit the monster, it fell back, and began to glow again. Its form turned molten, and started to melt back into a glowing blob. Then it started to shrink.

"I knew it!" I shouted triumphantly. "This monster is just a decoy that the true monster threw out at us to shield itself! My own monster used to do the same thing!"

"Then…then what *is* the true monster?" Timmy asked.

"I, um…" I mumbled, as the light from my RevealeR suddenly began to flicker.

"I think *I* know," Jeannine said. And with that she stepped forward and lifted her RevealeR. Her light was strong and bright, far brighter than mine, and when it fell on the monster, it shrieked, and its shrinking, molten form shriveled and began to surge violently. But the glow surrounding it grew stronger, and the blob started slowly dissolving back into the light. Jeannine smiled.

"This monster-fighting stuff is no big deal," she said. "My drama coach makes me work harder than this."

But at that very moment, Timmy shuddered, lifting a finger to point at the glowing mass.

"L...look," he whispered. "S-something's happening..."

And he was right. Behind the shrinking squirming blob, a new form began to take shape within the light. Just then, the shrill, echoing monster-voice erupted around us once more.

"NO, YOUR FATHER CAN'T COME TO THE PHONE AT THE MOMENT," it shrieked.

"HE'S...*BUSY* RIGHT NOW."

"You put him on! I want to talk to him!" We heard Timmy cry out.

Only it *wasn't* Timmy. Jeannine and I turned and looked right at him, but he was completely frozen, and hadn't uttered a word.

"You put him on right now!" insisted Timmy's voice.

"That...that's Timmy's voice," Jeannine said. "But where is it coming from?"

"Hel*lo* Jeannine," I grumbled. "It's not coming from me, you, or Timmy. Where do you *think* it's coming from?"

"You mean," she gasped. "It's coming *from the monster itself?*"

"Obviously," I said impatiently. "The real question is *WHY?* Why does the monster think that hearing that will be frightening?"

"Um..." Jeannine stuttered. "I think we may be about to find out. *Look.*"

Jeannine pointed over my shoulder, and I turned back to look at the glowing blob. As we watched, a shimmering figure began to emerge.

Chapter Nine - Breakdowns

"Something…" Timmy stuttered as he reached out and tugged on my sleeve. "Something is coming…"

"I can see that!" I grumbled irritably as I pulled loose from his grasp and turned to face the figure emerging from the glowing mass. The dazzling form was smaller than Timmy's father had been, but was more radiant, with sparkles of light shimmering all over.

"Wow…" I mumbled in an almost trance-like voice, "It's so…beautiful." But just then Timmy grabbed my arm again. When I looked back and saw the horror on his face, I remembered where I was, and what I was facing. Without another word, I lifted my RevealeR and pointed it at the shimmering form. The aura around it immediately began flickering, and the glow began to fade, growing softer and softer until at last the figure within was revealed.

It was a woman. Not a horrible, monster-looking kind of woman, mind you. A *gorgeous* woman. She was tall, blond, and perfectly tan, wearing a glittery gold halter top, a short black skirt, fancy high-heel shoes, and lots of big flashy jewelry.

"That's it?" I wondered out loud. "Your monster is some kind of a…a fashion model? What are you afraid she'll do, give you a makeover?"

But both Jeannine and Timmy were positively horrified. I stared in disbelief at their eyes, which were wide and frozen with fear.

"I don't…" I muttered as I gazed from one terror-stricken face to the other, "I don't get it…"

Don't be mad at Will, Jeannine had told Timmy. *He just doesn't know what it's like.*

"Bigelow said I need to understand the monster to make the RevealeR work," I whispered to myself. "But what can I do if I don't…"

But at that very moment, my eyes caught sight of the RevealeR in Jeannine's hand, whose bright beam was pointing uselessly at the ceiling.

"Of course!" I shouted, and then ran over to Jeannine and shook her arm hard until I drew her eyes over to mine. "Jeannine! Shine your light on the monster! It has to be *you* that does it!"

"What difference will that make?" she growled angrily, pulling her arm away.

"It makes all the difference!" I insisted. "I don't fully understand the monster, so I can't really see it the way Timmy does. But *you* do. We need your light! You have to show me what the monster looks like to you!"

Jeannine glared at me, but then turned her gaze back to the monster, and her face hardened. She lifted her RevealeR and pointed the beam right at the monster in high-heel shoes. But instead of brightening, the monster's face suddenly grew dark, and its features turned stiff and sharp.

"That's it!" I shouted. "I'm finally starting to see!"

But what I started to see was horrible. The shimmering, golden curls on her head turned filthy and shaggy, and spiked horns sprouted from her newly weed-like hair. Her fingers stretched longer and became rigid, pointy talons, and her arms turned dark and scaly. Her body melted and morphed into the shape of a demonic gargoyle.

"It…" I stuttered. "It's a…a *HARPY*!"

As I watched, the monster lifted her hand and the telephone receiver floated into her grasp, and then a voice, shrill and full of venom, erupted into the air.

"I TOLD YOU, HE'S BUSY!" the monster said smugly into the receiver. "I'LL HAVE HIM CALL YOU BACK WHEN HE CAN."

Then she gave a huge, twisted, evil grin.

"OR, WILL I?" she added, and then cackled a hideous, shrieking laugh. I gasped when her open mouth revealed a slithering, serpent tongue, and rows of shark-like teeth.

"NO!" Timmy cried out. I looked at Timmy

to be sure it was really him talking.

"NO! You can't have him! He's mine!" Timmy cried.

"OH, REALLY?" the monster said. She produced from behind her back her other hand, which she opened to reveal a six-inch high figure of...

"Dad! Daddy!" Timmy cried. "Don't let her! Don't let her take you!"

I looked at Jeannine, whose hands began shaking. The monster giggled, dropped the receiver, and then took Timmy's father and began twisting and turning him like he was made of silly putty. She stretched and pulled and then finally wrapped him around her little finger, prodding his head so that it bounced up and down like a bungee ball. Jeannine let out a huge sob, then dropped her flashlight and fell whimpering to the floor. Timmy cowered, and the monster, no longer bathed in the light of Jeannine's RevealeR, began to grow. She quickly towered over me, and her claw-like fingers poised to strike.

"Um, guys, I could use a little help here..." I whispered as the monster rose above me.

"NOW THEN, WHERE WAS I?" the monster posed. "AH, YESSSSS..."

And with that, she let out an ear-piercing shriek, unfurled a pair of bat-like wings, and took to the air. She hovered briefly, then plunged at me, swiping her claws viciously. I dove aside in the nick of time. The monster let out a shrieking laugh.

"Timmy!" I shouted. "You have to stand up to it! You have to face it, Timmy!"

But Timmy and Jeannine continued cowering, and did not get up.

It's no use, I thought. *He's too scared. We all are.*

Things were looking pretty bad, but at just that moment, I heard Bigelow's voice once more in the back of my head.

Remember, Will: things are always less scary when you face them with a friend.

He…he didn't mean himself, I realized. *He meant **us**. He meant NOW!*

"Timmy! Jeannine!" I shouted as I ran over to them. "Grab hold! Grab hold of my flashlight!"

I held it out to them, but they still cowered.

"Jeannine!" I pleaded. "Jeannine, grab hold! We can only beat this thing together!"

She looked up at me with tearstained eyes.

"I...I can't, Will!" she cried. "You were right. I'm not brave enough. I'm just a *girl*."

"You *are* brave! And you were right! You were right all along! I *need* you! We all need each other! We can be braver together!"

I pushed the flashlight toward her, and she tentatively reached for it. When she touched it, the beam grew stronger. Jeannine looked up at me, and I nodded. She grabbed hold firmly.

"Now you, Timmy!" I called out. "We all have to do this together!"

Timmy whimpered, but Jeannine reached out to him, and touched him gently on the shoulder. He looked at her, and her calm face drew him closer. Together, Jeannine and I held out the light to him, and he took hold. Just then...

"WELL, WHAT HAVE WE HERE?" the shrieking harpy bellowed. "FRESH MEAT?!" And she flew right at us.

"Stay cool," I instructed. "Breathe deeply to help control your fears, and focus showing this witch for what she really is!"

And we did. The three of us stood together, holding fast to my RevealeR, and pointed it true.

The monster screamed. She dropped from the air and began writhing on the floor, shriveling and shrinking as she hissed and snapped at us. The figure of Timmy's father, which still dangled in the palm of her claw, unraveled, and began to grow. In seconds, it was larger than the monster that held it, whose grip on him weakened in the glow from the RevealeR.

"Yes!" Timmy cheered.

"It's working!" Jeannine shouted. "Will, you're doing it!"

"*We're* doing it," I corrected. "Together, we have enough bravery and understanding to finally reveal the truth about this monster!"

And even as I spoke, a monster's voice erupted into the air around us. But the voice was not a screech or shriek anymore.

"He hates me," a soft, echoing woman's voice moaned. "Your son hates me."

"He doesn't hate you," a calm, though exasperated sounding man's voice resounded in reply. Timmy stiffened at the sound of the voice.

"He *hates* me," the woman's voice continued. "Every time I answer the phone…"

"Give the kid a break," the man coaxed. "He's had a really tough time with all that's been going on."

"Dad!" Timmy whispered as a slow smile crept onto his face. "Dad, you…you stood up for me!"

And though neither of the figures before us seemed to notice, the change in Timmy's mood strengthened the beam from the RevealeR, and its slightly greenish color turned to blue. Then, as the scene continued playing out, the monsters slowly shrank.

"*He's* had a tough time?" The woman cried out, and for a moment a bit of the terrible screeching sound returned to her voice. "What about *me*? I never asked for any of this! I never asked for all of these complications and problems and sticky situations!"

As the voice rang out, the tiny harpy tried to slash and tear at the figure of Timmy's father, but her talons had no effect. She hissed and clawed at him, but he remained firm and impassive.

"Like it or not, you *chose* all that when you chose to be with me," Timmy's father countered. "But Timmy didn't get to choose, yet his whole world has been turned upside-down. And it's all been too much for him."

"So that makes it OK for him to treat me like…like some horrible creature?" the woman hissed.

"Look, what do you think I can do?" Timmy's dad protested. "We're already sending him to a therapist. What more do you want?"

"I want him to stop hating me!" the woman cried. "I want him to…"

"He doesn't hate you," the man insisted. "He doesn't even know you. All he sees is a woman who broke up his family and stole away his daddy."

"*What?!* I hadn't even *met* you then!" the woman shouted indignantly. "I didn't have anything to do with you and your wife breaking up!"

"I know that," Timmy's father said impatiently. "But Timmy doesn't. Not yet. But he'll come around. He's a good kid. Just give it time."

Just give it time. Those words bounced around the room, and Timmy grew stronger, and his posture grew straighter with every echo. As Timmy firmed, the monsters weakened and shrank more, until they were the size of two action figures.

"You see, Timmy?" I coaxed. "Just keep facing them! In the light of truth, the monsters can't hurt you."

But at that very moment, the doll-sized harpy turned from the image of Timmy's father and faced us once more, her fangs still bared and vicious.

"OH, YOU THINK SO?" the tiny figure taunted. Her voice, unlike the soft woman's voice that had spoken to Timmy's father, was again a monstrous shriek. "YOU DON'T THINK I HAVE A FEW TRICKS LEFT?"

A sudden surge of burning heat shot through my hand where it gripped the RevealeR, and a reddish burst flared through its beam. I looked up at Timmy, and I saw anger blazing in his eyes. I just turned my gaze back to the harpy and kept the RevealeR pointed at her, steady and sure, and she continued shrinking.

"THERE'S MORE TO FEAR THAN JUST LITTLE OLD ME, ISN'T THERE?" the demon woman teased as she shrank. "WOULDN'T YOU AGREE, TIMMY?"

"Huh!" I said smugly. "I wonder what she meant by that?"

Just then, Jeannine stomped on my foot again.

"Yeeoooww!" I yelled. "What do you think you're doing?"

But Jeannine just pointed behind me, and when I turned around, my mouth dropped open.

There, hovering over by the desk, was the ring. Only it wasn't a little, slip-onto-your-finger golden band any more. It was huge, bigger than a beach ball, and still swelling enormously. In just seconds, it was bigger than Timmy's mattress-fort.

"It…it's growing," I muttered.

"Duh, Sherlock," Jeannine hissed.

"But…but why?" I wondered. "It's just a ring!"

I pulled my RevealeR away from Jeannine and Timmy and shined its light on the ring, but it had no effect. The ring kept growing, and as it did, it rose above us, continuing to expand in the empty space over our heads. It quickly filled the room, stretching almost from wall to wall.

"What is it doing…?" I started to say. But before I could utter even one more word, the ring dropped down, descending until it completely surrounded us.

"Noooooooo!" Timmy wailed. "No, let me

go!"

"There's no way out!" I shouted as I whirled around, shining my RevealeR in every direction. "We're trapped!"

I spun completely around, but my light revealed nothing but the shimmering inner walls of the ring until finally it caught in its beam another glowing blob. It was much like the first two, except that its oblong form was horizontal, and it felt somehow stronger, with bright, glowing sparkles that throbbed with power. At least, that's how it appeared to *me*.

"That looks like…" Jeannine whispered as she rummaged through her pocket for her glasses and threw them on. "Oh! Oh, *no*!"

"What?" I urged. "What is it?"

But before she could answer, headless fangs suddenly sprouted from the surrounding walls and took monstrous bites at the air all around us, forcing us to dodge and retreat.

"Hey, Mr. Monster Detective!" Timmy cried as he jumped and sidestepped the flying teeth. "What do we do *now*?"

"Um, I'm working on it!" I shouted as I ducked a set of snapping jaws.

To be perfectly honest, at that moment I was running kind of low in the ideas department. But though I was at a loss for what to do next, Jeannine's face turned resolute.

"*I'll* show this monster that it can't...uh, wait," she shouted, but then began feeling around her clothes frantically for something in her pocket that was not there. "Oh, this stupid dress! Where's my flashlight?"

"The same place as everything else you lose!" I hollered. "It's right in front of you!"

Jeannine looked down and spotted her yellow flashlight on the ground, lying where she had dropped it earlier. She reached to grab it, but several sets of fangs snapped at her, driving her back. Suddenly, long, slimy tentacles grew from the wall behind Jeannine, and they reached to snare her.

"No!" I cried, and leaped between Jeannine and the tentacles, which then grabbed me like an octopus. I struggled against those slimy arms, but one of them wrapped itself around my leg, and the next thing I knew, it had hoisted me right off the ground and hung me upside down like side of beef in a meat locker.

"Oh, how do I get myself into these things?" I grumbled as a pair of vicious, fanged jaws came flying right at my face.

That's right, this is where my story started. But if you think that how I ended up like that makes for a strange story, believe me, things were still just getting interesting.

"Will! Look out!" Jeannine shouted as I swayed back and forth, dodging and swiping at the incoming jaws.

"Just get the light!" I yelled back as I smacked one set of fangs with the casing of my RevealeR. But just then, another tentacle reached to grab her.

"No! Get back!" I heard Timmy's voice shout as he jumped in and flailed and fought with the advancing arm. He looked around frantically and spotted something perched against a stack of books nearby.

"My hockey stick!" he roared. "Perfect!"

He dashed over and grabbed it, then began swinging it wildly at the tentacles and the flying jaws. He smacked one pair of fangs right into next week.

"Ha!" He shouted. "Gotcha!"

But even as he spoke, more tendrils began sprouting, and it was just a matter of time before they ensnared us all. Jeannine looked back at me desperately.

"Go!" I shouted.

Give Jeannine credit, she didn't hesitate. She ducked under the tentacles, dodged the snapping teeth, and dove to grab her RevealeR. She picked it up, and sighed.

"Well, that's more like it…"

But before she could finish her sentence, one of the tendrils grabbed her, and lifted her upside down off the floor, making her dress hang down over her face.

"Jeannine, use the light!" I called out as a pair of fangs bit into my jacket and began shaking me, drawing me closer to those hideous teeth.

"I can't!" she moaned as she tried to push her dress back up her legs. "You'll…you'll see my panties!"

"*Jeannine*!" I shouted. "I'm getting *eaten* here!" My right arm and my one free leg were braced against the slobbering fangs, straining to prevent them from snapping shut on me.

"Oh, all right!" she grumbled, her voice slightly muffled by the portion of her dress that had floated in front of her face. She flicked on the switch.

The light came on, and when Jeannine pointed it at the walls of the giant ring, the sound of screeching instantly filled the air. Then the tendrils began to melt, and the snapping jaws withdrew back into the wall.

"Yeeeooow!" I cried as the dissolving tentacle dropped me, and I fell just like a sack of potatoes. Except potatoes don't get bruised when they land on their heads. Meanwhile, the tentacle holding Jeannine let her down gently before fading away.

"Girls always have it easier," I grumbled as I

rubbed the swelling lump on the back of my skull.

"Oh, stop whining," Jeannine retorted. "It was only your head."

I glared at her, but Jeannine's eyes were fixed upon the melting, morphing inner walls of the ring, which flattened, and grew taller, until they looked like the inside of a doll's house. I began staring at them too, but waves of screeching noises kept buffeting my ears, and I finally turned to find their source. It seemed that they were coming from the glowing, oblong blob, but when I pointed my RevealeR at it, nothing happened.

"This makes no sense," I said, noticing as I spoke that my light had dimmed once more. "We uncovered the truth about Timmy's monster, and he faced it. The harpy lost her power. So what is this? I just don't get it."

"Don't you?" Jeannine chided, as she glanced down her nose at me with an annoying *I know something you don't know* look on her face. "Look again."

And then she turned the beam of her RevealeR to the glowing blob. At first, nothing seemed to happen.

"OK," I muttered. "What am I supposed to be seeing, exactly?"

But Timmy went nuts. He held his ears and began swinging around like he was being whipped from every direction.

"Nooooooo!" he shouted. "Make it stop!"

That was when I realized that even though what I was seeing hadn't changed, what I was *hearing* had.

"The screeching..." I whispered. "It's changed. It's more of a...a wail..."

"It's *crying*," Jeannine corrected.

I grimaced at her.

"Crying?" I sputtered. "The monster is *crying*? What kind of monster...?"

Then, like a ton of bricks, it hit me. The light of my RevealeR suddenly burned bright again. I knew.

"It...it can't be..."

But as I waved the beam of my RevealeR around the room, everything began coming into focus. The walls of the ring were no longer just a glowing blur. The details became sharp, and decorations began coming into view: lacy curtains, turquoise and pink wallpaper with patterns of bears and bunnies, and in the corner of the room, a rocking horse. I turned the beam back to the oblong blob, and its glow faded, and finally the true monster became clear.

Chapter Ten – Growing Pains

It looked like a small, topless cage on stilts. Along the inside of the bars ran a frilly white bumper that blocked any view of what was within. The sides rustled as though something inside was shaking back and forth.

"A crib?" I puzzled. "The monster is a..."

At just that moment, another deafening wail roared at us, so loud that the crib and surrounding furniture shook like they were in an earthquake. I struggled to keep my balance, but after I righted myself and saw what had caused the noise, my knees started shaking from the *inside*.

You see, the sides of the crib rustled once more, only this time, something reached out. A huge hand, petite and swollen like a baby's, but grime-covered and purplish with horrid scales and spines, rose into view above the top of the bumper.

"Eeeuuuuuuww!" Jeannine sputtered disgustedly. "Don't monsters believe in personal hygiene?"

Just then a sharp, piercing cry rang out that rattled the walls.

"FEED ME!" it shrieked.

And with that, there was a harsh tearing noise as the bumper around the crib was shredded into a gazillion pieces. Then something behind the shreds arose. I say *something* because I honestly couldn't guess what it was. It looked like a giant, beaten-up soccer ball that had fallen into a toxic waste dump. But then it rotated toward me, and two horrid, bulging red eyes stared down at us. Its nose was just a moss-covered stump, and its mouth was barely visible through the goo that covered the entire head, until it opened, revealing massive, slime-covered fangs.

"FEED ME!" the thing in the crib bellowed.

I looked over at Timmy.

"Um, do you still have those chocolate bars?" I asked weakly.

Timmy just whimpered. The monster didn't wait for us to respond. Its horrible mouth cracked open wide, and a froglike tongue shot out in our direction.

"Look out!" I shouted as I lunged at Jeannine and shoved her aside. We dove down, and the tongue soared past us and flew straight at Timmy.

"Timmy, *move!*" I yelled. But he just stood there frozen like a deer in headlights. The tongue snared the end of Timmy's hockey stick, and then yanked it right out of his hands and pulled it back to the monster-baby's mouth. Its horrible jaws snapped the stick in two, and then drew it into its mouth, where it began noisily chewing. Once the stick was gone, the monster let out a thunderous belch, and the entire room vibrated.

"FEED ME!" it said again, looking down at Timmy hungrily like he was a giant Hershey Bar.

"Timmy!" I called to him. "Timmy, snap out of it!"

But he just stared blankly at the monster as its tongue shot out again. But this time the tongue wasn't aimed at Timmy. Instead, it snared the doll-sized figure of Timmy's father.

"No, let me go!" the figure howled. It struggled and squirmed helplessly as the tongue drew it toward those horrible, grinding teeth. Timmy moaned a wail of despair.

"Noooooo!" he cried, finally breaking out of his stupor and running over to the tiny figure of his father. He grabbed hold of one arm and began pulling, trying to yank his father loose, but the strength of the monster was too much for him, and he was dragged along with his father toward those terrible jaws.

"Jeannine!" I called out desperately. "Jeannine, use your light! I need to see what Timmy is really up against!"

"But I *am* using my light!" she shouted back.

"What?!" I bellowed, turning my head to look at her. Sure enough, she was right next to me, RevealeR in hand, with its beam pointed squarely at the monsters.

"But this makes no sense!" I protested.

"Doesn't it?!" Jeannine hollered impatiently.

"Come on, Jimmy Neutron, boy genius! Figure it out!"

"You know I hate when people call me that!" I complained. "Can't you just use your light to show me what this looks like to you?"

"I *am* showing you!" she insisted.

"You...*are*...?" I mumbled. And I turned back to the monsters again.

Timmy was still tugging desperately at his father's arm, trying to pull him loose, while the doll sized figure's legs were bracing against the side of the crib, fighting the pull of the tongue that drew him relentlessly toward those crushing jaws.

"No!" Timmy cried out. "No, he's *mine*!"

But still the tongue dragged both of them ever closer.

"Stop!" the figure of Timmy's father cried out. "Let go! I have to go to Timmy!"

"NO GO TO TIMMY!" the monster yelled. "DADDY MUST FEED ME!"

"Of...of course," I whispered to myself. My light instantly grew strong once more.

"You get it now?" Jeannine asked.

"Yes," I said.

And with that, I pointed my RevealeR at the monster and shined the light right in its face. Instantly, its fangs and red eyes melted away.

"That's it!" I cheered. "Now I've...wait, something's wrong..."

Something *was* wrong. Really, *really* wrong. The monster wasn't shrinking at all. And even though its fangs were gone, the monstrous frog-like tongue remained, and continued to draw the figure of Timmy's father, kicking and screaming, to its mouth.

"Nooooo! Stop!" Timmy's father pleaded as his feet began to slide into the baby's jaws. "Stop this! Timmy needs me!"

But he kept sliding in deeper. Timmy braced himself against the crib and pulled desperately on the arm of his father, struggling to tear him from the baby's jaws.

"What's going on?" I cried. "My RevealeR is having no effect!"

Mine neither!" Jeannine shrieked. "Why isn't it working?"

"Noooooo!" Timmy screamed as the monster sucked his father's legs into its mouth and continued chewing. "Let go!"

Then his eyes turned to me.

"Help me!" he begged. "Please, *help*!"

I watched Timmy struggling to pull his father free, and smacked my flashlight in frustration.

"Why won't it work?" I wondered helplessly.

It was then that I remembered my talk with Bigelow, and what I had learned about the RevealeR.

It shines light on monsters. It shows what they really are, and makes them less scary.

"It shows what the monsters really are," I whispered. "The RevealeR shows what Timmy is really scared of."

"What?" Jeannine said.

"Jeannine! I've got it! The light reveals the truth about Timmy's fear! That's what it does!"

"Yes," Jeannine muttered. "So what?"

"Well," I answered, "What if this *is* the truth?"

Jeannine gave me a *you've lost your mind* kind of look.

"The truth?" she said. "Timmy's afraid that his dad will be eaten by a baby monster is the truth?"

"No! But what if Timmy's father doesn't have much time for him anymore? Maybe his dad really is being taken from him!"

"By a baby?" Jeannine wondered.

"It's possible, isn't it?" I posed.

"*Possible*? Well, sure!" she said caustically. "I mean, *anything's* possible..."

Suddenly, Jeannine's eyes lit up. She looked down at her flashlight, and it grew brighter.

"Of course..." she whispered to herself. Then she turned back to me and bellowed, "Will! You said the RevealeR turns truth into light, right?"

"Right! But that's not doing us any good..."

"Well, there's more than just *one* truth possible here! Maybe we can use the RevealeR to make Timmy see *another* truth! Let's show him a different possibility."

"And how do we do that?"

Jeannine bit her lip for a moment, then without another word she pointed her flashlight at the baby and closed her eyes.

"Take hold!" she commanded.

I hate when she gets all bossy like that, but it was the only plan going, so I did what she said.

"OK!" I grumbled. "Now what?"

"Now close your eyes and try to think of something nice about having a new baby in your family!" she instructed.

"What? Why?" I asked.

Jeannine shook her head impatiently. I'm pretty sure that she rolled her eyes under her closed eyelids too.

"Will," she said. "You told me that when we understand something, the RevealeR makes light so everyone can see it, right?"

"Right! Then we all see what you see."

"Well then, if we understand that there are other possibilities than this one," she explained, "maybe the light can show *them* to Timmy too."

For a moment, my mouth hung open stupidly. But at least I didn't drool.

"That...that's brilliant, Jeannine!" I gushed. "Let's try it!"

And so I closed my eyes and tried to imagine how much fun it would be to be a big brother. Unfortunately, the only images that came to my mind were of wailing babies, trashed toys, and poopy diapers.

"Um, I'm kind of drawing a blank here," I confessed. "Have *you* thought of anything? Anything *good* I mean?"

"I think so!" Jeannine called out. "Is it working?"

"I don't know," I replied. "Let me check."

And with that, I opened my eyes.

"Oh, wow..." I whispered.

For there in front of me, the monster nursery had begun to melt again. The crib, the curtains, the rocking horse...*everything* was glowing warmly, and the walls started turning back into hazy blobs.

"You're doing it, Jeannine! You're..." I cheered, but she just waved me off.

"Hush!" she commanded. "I'm focusing on making a picture in my mind. I've got to concentrate!"

Meanwhile, Timmy was still yanking hard on the arm of the doll-sized version of his dad, when suddenly it evaporated, and he went flying into a stack of books. The stack collapsed on top of him, burying him in old almanacs and atlases.

"Help!" he cried. "They're all over me!"

"Take it easy," I instructed as I let go of Jeannine's RevealeR and hurried over to dig him out. "You're covered in books, not monsters."

"There's a difference?" he asked as I put my flashlight in my pocket and helped him get up.

Right then I realized why Timmy gets such lousy grades.

"No wonder you need a math tutor..." I said scornfully, but then I saw his face, which was staring at a spot directly behind me and had frozen in shock.

"Uh, oh," I mumbled.

I whipped my RevealeR back out of my pocket and spun around, but then *I* froze in shock too.

Standing on the floor beside the crib, bathed in the hazy, amber glow from Jeannine's RevealeR, was *another* Timmy. I did a double take, turning from the figure beside the crib to Timmy, who was still frozen beside me, and then back again. They were exactly the same, but for the fact that the Timmy by the crib didn't have drool all over himself and smelled a lot better.

"What is that?" Timmy finally stuttered. I just looked at him, and then back at Jeannine. She was standing exactly as I had left her, eyes closed and perfectly still, with a look of deep concentration on her face. The bright beam of the RevealeR in her hand was fixed directly on the figure standing by the crib.

"This must be *it*," I replied as my eyes followed the beam of light back to the figure of Timmy. "This must be the image she made in her mind! We're really seeing it!"

"This is Jeannine's image...of *me*?"

Just as Timmy spoke, the phantom-like figure that looked like him moved in closer to the crib. He leaned over the railing and then waved his fingers, puffed out his cheeks, and began making funny faces.

"Ah Booga Booga Boo!" he said. The real Timmy watched this and grimaced.

"But...but I look ridiculous!" Timmy protested.

"About time you noticed," I snickered.

Suddenly, the sound of a baby's laughter echoed around us. The figure of Timmy chortled.

"Ah Booga Booga Boo!" he said again, and laughter erupted once more.

I smiled, but when I looked at the *real* Timmy, his face had the same look of horror and humiliation that mine had the day my mom visited our school and gave me a big, red kiss on the cheek in front of my entire gym class.

"Jeannine!" I cried out. "This one's not helping! Try thinking of something else!"

"OK," she called back. "How about this...?"

And then the light from her RevealeR blazed bright, and for a second I shielded my eyes with my hand. Then the light faded, and I gazed around.

At first glance, the room hadn't changed, but then I looked down, and saw that toys littered the floor.

"Well, if *Timmy* doesn't wig out about this," I commented, "I'll bet his *mom* will."

Then I turned back to the crib, but it was *gone*. Instead, there was the other Timmy again, this time sitting reading a storybook to a small child in a striped shirt and blue overalls that sat beside him.

"...And they all lived happily ever after," he read. As he turned the page, the child smiled up at him and grasped his arm affectionately. I looked over at the real Timmy, and saw his lip quiver.

"That...that's so *nice*," he stuttered. "But still, that little thing is so...*disgusting*."

"What?" I sputtered. "How can you possibly call that cute little...?"

But then I stopped myself, because I remembered

how I had seen the ring as just a tiny piece of gold, but Timmy saw a terrifying monster.

Timmy's not seeing what I see, I realized. *We still see things differently.*

"Well?" Jeannine called out.

"Nice try, Jeannine," I told her. "But Timmy still isn't convinced. The baby still looks like a monster to him. What else have you got?"

Jeannine opened her eyes and glared at me. Even without her eyes closed, the images she created remained.

"Why don't *you* think of something?" she growled.

"I can't," I said. "I already tried!"

"Oh, come on, Will!" Jeannine urged. "Is it really so hard to imagine something nice about having a little brother?"

"A…little *brother*…?" I stuttered. Somehow, I hadn't thought of it that way. But once I did, a whole host of images flooded into my brain. I closed my eyes and focused on one of them, and felt the RevealeR grow warm and bright in my hand. Then I opened them again, and squinted a bit until the scene in front of me became clear.

There was the phantom Timmy, sitting on the floor face to face with a little boy. They were both wearing baseball caps and jerseys, and each was holding a stack of baseball cards. They took turns flipping their cards, and then the little boy cried out, "Yay! I win!" And then he picked up the cards.

"Is this for keepsies?" the boy asked. "Can I put these on my pile?"

"Why don't we make a *new* pile," the phantom Timmy answered. "A pile for both of us. Then we can share them all."

"OK," the child said, then he held up one of the cards he had won and looked it over.

"Who's this one?" he asked.

"That's Barry Bonds," the phantom Timmy said. "Lots of people don't like him, but I think he's the best ever."

"No, *you're* the best ever," the little boy said sweetly. The phantom Timmy smiled. I looked back at the real Timmy, and he was smiling too. As his smile grew broad and warm, the darkness in the room fell back, and the fear drained from his face. For the very first time, Timmy looked at the image of his future little brother with no horror, disgust, or anger in his eyes, and I was certain that he must finally be seeing the little monster the same as I did. Somehow, I knew that meant the moment of truth had finally come.

"Timmy," I said to him. "It's time. You know what you have to do, don't you?"

He looked back at me.

"Yes," he said.

I led him over to the two figures that sat on the floor bathed in the glow of the RevealeRs. The phantom-child looked up at Timmy.

"Who are you?" the little boy asked.

Timmy reached down and put his hand gently on the boy's shoulder.

"I'm Timmy," he answered. "I...I'm your brother."

The child reached up its arms to Timmy. Timmy hesitated a moment.

"Go on," I whispered.

Timmy smiled weakly, and then reached out and wrapped his arms around the child. The moment they embraced, the entire monster-nursery erupted with light, as bright and warm as the sun. The nursery walls floated back up over our heads and began to collapse into the center of the room. The furniture and toys glowed brightly and quickly shrank. As they did, some invisible magnet-like pull set them sliding toward the glowing figures of Timmy and his little brother. Then the phantom images of Timmy and his brother shrank too. In mere moments, the whole nursery was no larger than a doll's house.

"Look!" Jeannine said. "Up there."

Directly above our heads, the walls had melted back into the shape of a small golden ring. The ring pulsed with energy, then all of a sudden sparkling flares once again began shooting out from the center of its glowing form.

"Timmy, *duck*!" Jeannine cried as a flare flew past his head. But Timmy stood firm.

"No," he said firmly. "No more. No more hiding."

And just as he spoke, the flares sputtered and the glow surrounding the ring weakened. The ring shot out another blazing spear in Timmy's direction, but he didn't duck, or even flinch.

"Timmy!" Jeannine cried.

But the flame sputtered out and died before it even reached him. Then, after one last fluttering spurt, the glimmer surrounding it died, and the smoldering ring fell from the air into Timmy's waiting hand.

"Good work, Timmy!" I said, patting him on the back.

Meanwhile, the rest of the nursery kept shrinking until it was roughly the size of a paperweight. The air froze solid around the tiny scene, making it look like a snow globe, minus all the snow. Inside the frosty sphere, the image of the nursery, with Timmy and his little brother sitting together, remained.

. Timmy picked it up, and smiled at it. Then he turned to Jeannine and me.

"Thanks," he simply said.

And with that, the rest of the darkness flew from the room, replaced by the hazy glare of moonlight.

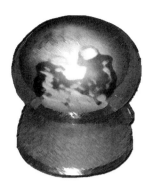

Chapter Eleven ~ Rewards

Timmy walked over and placed his new paperweight on his desk. Then he turned to us and opened his hand to reveal a simple golden band.

"It's your dad's wedding ring, isn't it?" Jeannine asked.

"Yes," Timmy said. "I found it in the drawer of his nightstand when I was looking for his new phone number."

I stepped up and looked over the ring with my MonsterScope. The glow, the pulsing energy, the

flares; they were all gone. It was just a ring.

"It's clean," I announced. "There's nothing monstrous about it at all anymore."

"Oh, I wouldn't say that," Jeannine stated as she too glanced over the ring. "I think your MonsterScope may have missed something."

I froze.

"What is it?" I asked. "What do you see?"

"Can't you see it?" she answered. "That horrible paisley pattern engraved into the gold? It's hideous!"

I exhaled deeply and frowned. Bigelow was definitely right when he said that things are less scary when you face them with a friend, but he forgot to mention that certain friends can really get on your nerves sometimes.

"All right, enough of that," I declared. "You've got some explaining to do."

"You mean about how I knew what the monster was?" Jeannine asked.

"No, about those Powerpuff Girls panties you wear."

Jeannine's eyes bugged worse than the time I told her she'd tucked her skirt into her tights, and then she got very stern.

"If you ever mention that to *anyone*…"

"Don't worry," I assured her. "You're secret's safe with us." I turned and looked over at Timmy and added, "*All* our secrets are safe. Monster

Detectives are sworn to secrecy. We're like doctors, except we don't stick you with needles or anything."

Timmy smiled, but Jeannine still looked a bit cross. I can't blame her: if I was caught wearing my Superman undershorts, I'd be pissy too.

Not that I'm admitting that I *have* Superman undershorts, mind you.

"Well, I expect you'll both be treating me with more respect from now on," she said firmly.

"Jeannine, I don't know what you're talking about," I protested. "I've *always* treated you with respect."

"You treat me," she said pointedly, "like a *girl.*"

"Well, if you want, from now on I'll treat you just like a boy."

"Hey, what about me?" Timmy complained. I looked back at him.

"Okay, I'll treat you just like a boy, too."

Jeannine smirked.

"Never mind," she said. "The world has too many boys as it is."

And with that, she turned and left the room. Timmy scowled at the door like he was shocked that she just up and left like that, but that's Jeannine for you.

"Now what did she mean by that?" Timmy whined.

I just shrugged.

"Girls," I said. "Who can figure them?"

Timmy's scowl broke, and he chuckled a bit.

"Yeah, you're right," he commented. "You know, my dad always says it doesn't even pay to try."

"That reminds me…" I started to say.

"…That you wanted to know more about the phone call I made to my dad?" Timmy guessed.

"No," I said. "It reminded me that I haven't been *paid*."

"Oh," Timmy said sheepishly. "Well, your business card says, '*fee negotiable*'. So what do you want?"

"I want a great big motorcycle with rocket boosters and lots of flashing lights," I answered.

I settled for the leftover chocolate bars.

The murky fog was slowly fading from the air by the time Jeannine and I left Timmy's house.

"Do come back again!" Timmy's mother called out in a sing-song voice as we trotted down the walkway.

"Wow! What got into her?" I said as we stepped through the gate.

But Jeannine didn't answer. In fact, she stayed silent for three whole blocks as I walked her home. I didn't know what to do, because that had never happened before, so I looked around aimlessly, then up at the night sky. It stretched black and endless in every direction, dotted here and there with only a few tiny points of light that struggled to reach us through the weakening fog. For some reason, I felt a sudden chill. I guess the quiet was making me nervous, so I pulled one of the chocolate bars out of my pocket and began eating. Now, Jeannine loves chocolate more than breathing, so when she didn't react to that, I knew something was really wrong. I took out my MonsterScope and checked her out, just to be sure that I was returning to Jeannine's mother her real daughter, and not some monster imitation. It *was* her of course, but then I looked at the spyglass itself, feeling badly that she didn't have one.

"So, I guess you're going to be a full-fledged detective after all," I told her. She blushed.

"Oh, I don't know," she said. "Maybe it'll be best if I just do the paperwork and stuff."

"What?" I said. "Why?"

Jeannine's eyes got a little teary.

"You're probably better off without me. I'm not a very good partner."

"What are you talking about? You're a *great…*"

"I left you, Will!" she suddenly cried. "I left you there to face the monsters alone!"

"But you came back," I answered. "And it was *you* that revealed the truth for all of us to see. I could never have done that without you."

"But I wasn't brave enough! You could have been eaten alive because of me!"

"Well actually, Bigelow told me that monsters don't really *eat* people..." I began, but as I did, Jeannine's face fell into her hands. Somehow, I could *feel* the guilt that was tormenting her, as real and alive as any monster, and I knew exactly what she needed.

"You know," I said gently, "the first time Bigelow told me to face my monster, I tried to run away."

Jeannine's face burst from her hands and she gasped like I had just told her I'd caught her mother, the strict vegetarian, eating pig's feet.

"You...you did?' she sputtered.

"I did. I think maybe that's something every monster detective has to go through. I mean, no one is born knowing how to face a monster, right? We all have to learn to do it. And you did that tonight."

Jeannine's scratched her head, and then her face changed into an *I'm thinking it over* expression.

"I *did*, didn't I?" she finally said.

"You did," I agreed.

Jeannine's face twitched for a moment, but then she finally nodded in agreement. But she still looked a little sad.

"But what about the next time?" she asked. "I mean, Bigelow *told* you that you should be a monster detective. How do we know *I'm* really cut out for this?"

"I don't know. Maybe..."

But I stopped speaking, because at that very

moment a sudden burning sensation began pressing against the side of my hip.

"Owww!" I growled. "What's going on?" And I reached into my scorching hot pants pocket and pulled out a small rectangular piece of paper. Instantly, the heat disappeared. I lifted the paper to my eyes and looked at it.

"What is that?" Jeannine asked.

"My business card," I answered. "The card that magically appears when people need me."

"But what is it doing here?" she asked.

I smiled broadly as I handed it to Jeannine.

"Take a look," I instructed.

Jeannine put on her glasses and held the card to her eyes.

It read:

"If the *card* says you're a detective," I said slyly, "Who are we to argue?"

Jeannine's face broke into a huge, bright smile.

"Well then," she said, straightening herself and resuming her normal, haughty tone of voice. "Does this mean I get a raise?"

"Sure," I answered, and broke her off an extra large piece of the chocolate bar. "Here you go."

She took it and began eating.

"But you still don't get the big flashlight," I told her.

Jeannine went to stomp my foot, but then stopped and gave me a gentle nudge instead.

"It's okay," she giggled. "I told you before: red really isn't my color." And then she blushed again, and proved it was true.

"So, Jeannine Fitsimmons," I called out in my T.V. announcer voice, "You've just helped solve our first case and been promoted to detective. What will you do now? Go to Disneyland?"

She giggled some more, but then straightened herself and cleared her throat.

"Actually," she said, "I think I'll use my new rank to take charge of any cases we get for the next week or so."

"Oh, you think so?" I said with a smirk. "And what makes you think *I'm* going to agree to that?"

"Oh, I don't think you have much of a choice," she said casually. "Seeing as how it's 8:30, and you're about to be grounded."

I looked at my watch. It read 8:32, which meant I was doomed. I handed her the MonsterScope.

"I guess I won't be needing this for a while," I said.

Jeannine giggled gleefully as she took it into her hands.

"Oooh!" she cooed as she looked it over. "I can't wait to show my mom! Just wait until she sees what this can do! She'll freak out!"

"Um, I don't think so, Jeannine," I said. "People can't really see what they don't understand, remember? I'm pretty sure grownups won't see anything but a plain old spyglass."

Jeannine's smile melted. She thought it over for a moment, then pulled out her RevealeR.

"Well, what about this?" she said. "Can I use it to make her see…you know, *scary* stuff?"

"It won't work on real moms and dads," I told her. "I already tried."

"Well, what about the monsters? Won't they…"

"Grownups can't see them," I said sadly. "They never understand."

Jeannine frowned.

"Well then," she sighed, "I guess they'll never believe that we're really doing anything at all."

"True," I agreed. "But then I suppose that's one of the hazards of running a monster detective agency."

Jeannine just looked at me and smiled.

"Well," she said, "at least this chocolate is

really good."

And we walked close together in the darkness the rest of the way home.

Kids!

Can't wait for more

Monster Detective Agency

adventures?

Never Fear!!

You can read more Monster Detective stories, and find Monster Games and Puzzles too on our website

MonsterDetectiveAgency.com !

It's FREE!

you can also find special messages from Will, read and leave comments on Jeannine's blog, get Monster-Fighting tips from Bigelow, and see a sneak preview of our next book!

Get your parents' permission, then check it out today!

Will's Tips For Fighting Monsters

1) Always face your monsters

Monsters hate this. They don't want you to face them because even though it may not seem like it right away, monsters start to shrink as soon as you see the truth about them.

2) Have backup

Like Bigelow says, we are always braver when we face our monsters with a friend. Anyone you trust will do. Having someone to lean on when things get scary is something no monster detective should be without.

3) Stay as calm as you can

Calming your body helps prevent fear (and the monsters) from growing stronger, and keeps your mind thinking clearly. One way to calm yourself is to practice deep breathing exercises, like the ones my mom used when I accidentally spilled paint all over her new carpet. Remember: monsters feed off of fear, so if we can control our fears, we take away their power over us. And monsters with no power won't want to hang around very much.

4)   Believe in yourself

It may seem silly, but sometimes you have to talk to yourself. Remind yourself that you can be brave and strong. Always remember that no matter how scary something looks or how small you feel, you are bigger on the INSIDE than any monster could ever be.

The adventure continues in

Will Allen and the

HIDEOUS SHROUD

In the next adventure of the Monster Detective Agency, Will discovers that even *creeps* have monsters. But when big, tough bully Duncan Williams is tormented by a monster that hides its face, will the secret under the mask be too much for Will to unravel when his client may be more threatening than the monster itself, and his RevealeR may have become more dangerous than the monsters?

Jason Edwards is an author, teacher, coach, and father, who possesses a B.S. in Psychology and a M.A. in Education. Jason has more than 20 years of experience helping children deal with their monsters.

To learn more about the author, you can visit him anytime on the web at his Facebook or MySpace pages, follow him on Twitter, read his latest blog at MonsterDetectiveAgency.com, or e-mail him at Jason@RogueBearPress.com. Jason always enjoys hearing from his readers and their parents (and always replies to their letters).